D1062523

MAN WITH A SWORD

Other books by Henry Treece
published by the Children's Book Department
of The Bodley Head

LEGIONS OF THE EAGLE
THE BURNING OF NJAL
VINLAND THE GOOD
VIKING'S DAWN
THE ROAD TO MIKLAGARD
VIKING'S SUNSET
THE EAGLES HAVE FLOWN

HENRY TREECE

Man with a Sword

Decorations by
WILLIAM STOBBS

THE BODLEY HEAD
LONDON SYDNEY
TORONTO

This book is for
J. B.

SBN 370 01211 9

© The Estate of Henry Treece, 1962
Illustrations © The Bodley Head Ltd, 1962
Printed and bound in Great Britain for
The Bodley Head Ltd
9 Bow Street, London, WC2
by C. Tinling & Co. Ltd, Prescot
Set in Monotype Plantin
First published 1962
This edition 1970

Contents

About this book, vii

PART ONE: 1041–1047

1. Holmgang, 3
2. Baldwin of Flanders, 12
3. Visitors from England, 18
4. King Swein's Figs, 25
5. Attack at Night, 31
6. Boar's Head Helmet, 35

PART TWO: 1047–1068

7. Hardrada's Judgement
   and the Melon, 49
8. Miklagard, 56
9. Bad News, 60
10. Earl Tostig, 63
11. Stamfordbridge, 69
12. Shield-Ring, 74
13. End of an Age, 77
14. Gay Bargain, 81
15. The Man in the Marsh, 84

PART THREE: 1068–1072

16. Black Bargain, 93
17. The Golden Borough, 97
18. The Fortress at Ely, 102
19. Departure and Attack, 104
20. The Ruined Causeway, 110
21. The New Enemy, 114
22. The New Causeway, 117
23. Escape, 119
24. Dungeon, 123

PART FOUR: 1072–1077

   25. Queen Matilda, 127
   26. Baron, 135
   27. A Man Alone, 140
   28. The Quarrel, 146
   29. The King's Letter, 150
   30. Cnut, 153
   31. The Affairs of Princes, 156

PART FIVE: 1077–1087

   32. Two Old Men, 163
   33. The Road to Normandy, 166
   34. The Priory of Saint Gervase, 169
   35. The Little Garden, 176

About this book

IT IS both fascinating and infuriating that we know so little about such a character as Hereward. The *Anglo-Saxon Chronicle* only mentions him twice. Under the year A.D. 1070: 'Then the monks of Peterborough heard say that their own men would plunder the minster; *namely Hereward and his company*. . . .' And under the year A.D. 1071: 'And the outlaws then all surrendered . . . *except Hereward alone*. . . .'

There are many legends, but few facts. His parentage seems to be quite unknown, though there are several incidental entries in the Domesday survey which connect him with the western edge of the Lincolnshire Fenland.

There is also the tradition that Hereward led the life of an outlaw in the once-forested district known as Bruneswald, in parts of Huntingdon and Northampton.

The historian, Sir Frank Stenton, assumes Hereward to have been 'a Lincolnshire thegn of moderate estate . . . who represents the spirit of Native resistance to the Conqueror.' And Hereward certainly seems to have resisted sufficiently to anger the Conqueror into saying, 'By God's Splendour . . . I will find . . . a man who will meet all his attacks.' So writes William of Malmesbury in 1125.

Florence of Worcester, writing a little earlier, tells of Hereward's escape from Ely; and, according to other chroniclers, he at last made peace with William the Conqueror.

Whatever the truth, Hereward does not seem to have appeared after the winter of 1085. In this story, however, I take the liberty of letting him live two years longer, so that he may be present at the death of his old enemy, King William.

It is always tempting to fill in the gaps of history. How did Hereward's career begin, one wonders. Reading William of Malmesbury, one finds that in 1041 Gunhilda, the English wife of the German Emperor, was insulted by a man 'of gigantic size'. Since no one would defend her against this giant, she sent over to

England for a young warrior, who fought her enemy and, 'through the miraculous interposition of God,' was able to ham-string him. Might not this young warrior have been Hereward?

HENRY TREECE

Part One

1041 - 1047

1. Holmgang

ALMOST A mile out of Bruges, in a crook of the river, lay a little green islet shaped like a fish. And rightly was it shaped, for boys fished there among the leaning alders in the summer, laughing and teasing the girls, and pushing each other into the shallow water as a joke or to show off to their sisters how strong they were.

Sometimes monks came there to walk up and down the grass and pray, or contemplate, or speak over the words of the blessed Saint Benedict. Often they had to drive the shouting boys off the islet with sticks, so as to get a little peace.

The boys would splash into the rippling water, naked as the day they were born, pretending to be afraid, but calling out, 'Baldheads! Baldheads! See if you can catch us now!'

The monks would pretend not to hear. With solemn faces they would gaze towards the grey roofs and towers of Bruges, then, signing themselves, would begin their meditation.

Once they used to chant, 'From the fury of the Northmen, good Lord defend us!' But now Northmen were everywhere, many of them grown very respectable, wearing decent clothes, speaking Flemish or Frankish, holding castles, even sitting on thrones.

There was no use in that prayer any more. God had defended Flanders in his own way—by making the Northmen see sense.

Even the little green islet was owned by a Northman, a baron named Odo. His grandfather, who sailed out of Hedeby, had called himself Odd—but that name was not delicate enough for a baron, so he got the Bishop to change it when he was baptized at the age of forty.

But the island was still known by its old Danish combat name, Holmganga, or 'going to the island', for men with quarrels to settle sometimes came with their swords, and many an argument had been finished there. The green grass had often been another colour; and old men said that heads had sometimes hung from the gnarled crab-apple tree.

Today, with the late sun slanting down across the towers of Bruges, casting a red glow over the flat fields and waterways, the islet was crowded with folk—all men, and most of them big raw-faced fellows who wore their hair long on to their shoulders, or plaited and then rolled into a bun at the nape of the neck.

Some wore iron helmets and short byrnies that only covered the chest. But none of them carried a sword or even as much as a dagger. And they were strangely silent, for the sort of men they were.

They stood round an enclosed space, watching thralls preparing it. In the middle was laid a square of stitched hide, ten feet along each of its edges. Round the hide they had scored three lines in the flat turf, one a foot beyond the other. At each corner of the last square they had set up hazel poles.

As one of the thralls drove in the last pole, sweating, he turned with his hand over his eyes to keep the sun out and said, 'Is this holmgang-field set right, Kormac?'

There was a big man lolling on a stool among the crowd. He was eating a chicken leg and drinking beer from a bull's horn. The iron byrnie on his broad chest was red with rust and tattered along its edges, the mail hanging down in shreds as though it had seen much service. His face was like a bull's, broad and hairy, with wide nostrils and rolling great eyes. Across his knees lay a sword,

4

hacked and bent, its blade mostly black with age. But the last nine inches, towards the point, were clean and sharp, glinting like old silver in the sun.

When the servant spoke this man looked up, the beer-horn at his lips, then nodded. He threw the chicken leg away, pushed the wooden stopper into the horn, then took his iron-hilted sword and began to stab it into the turf again and again, seeing how far he could bury the blade each time. Always it was nine inches, no more and no less.

A grey-haired man beside him said, 'Nine inches into the ground, two feet through a man, hey, Kormac?'

Kormac turned his head and gazed into the red sun, as though getting his eyes used to it. In a thick voice he said, 'I took this sword from a king's grave when I was first growing a beard. The witch-woman in my steading told me I should never drive it more than that into the ground. She said that when I drove it less than that, my friends should prepare a death-ship for me.'

The grey-haired man laughed and said, 'Then you will not be needing your ship today, Kormac. It seems the Englishman will give you no trouble.'

Kormac wiped the sword edge on the skirt of his linen tunic and said, 'It is just as well. I have been a paid killer for other men all my life, since I left home in Norway, yet today I haven't a bed to lie on—much less a ship to burn in!'

A youth whose face-hair was just coming, but who already wore a byrnie, called out, 'All men fear you, Kormac. That is worth more than a ship. There is a seat for you at every feast-hall. Your sword, Lang the long one, speaks louder for you than a king's herald does for him. You are rich.'

Kormac did not look at the boy. He said in his mumbling voice, 'Boys, women, and empty barrels—all sound, and nothing else. Go back to your father, Egil, and grow up to be a quiet farmer. A fighting-man's life is lonely; he cannot get a woman to marry him, he cannot have boys of his own, he cannot even have a bed to die in comfortably. He has nothing but his sword, and a few false friends to cheer him on when he is winning. They leave

5

him fast enough as soon as he takes a fall or two. Did you ever see men following a berserk who had lost his sword-hand?'

The youth said, 'I would follow you if you had no hands at all, for the hero that you once were. I would feed you and fight for you.'

Kormac looked over his shoulder and said to the grey-haired man, 'Take this boy away. He talks as though I am finished already. I hear Odin's ravens croaking in his voice. Send him home to his father. I do not want him near me.'

The men began to laugh, but they stopped when one of them called out, 'The Englishman is coming, look! His boat is full of men.'

Kormac gave the shallow boat a glance, then said, 'All men from the court, and that means no men. I can smell the scent they use from here. The woman, Gunhilda, seems to like pretty boys.'

The grey-haired man said, 'But it is not pretty boys you are fighting this day, Kormac. The Englishman is no courtier.'

Kormac was binding a broad strip of hide round his right wrist, paying great attention to it. He did not look up, but said, 'Describe him to me.'

The old man knew what this meant; he had tended fighting-men all his life, and had been one himself, before the sight of his right eye had gone. Fighting-men always pretended not to notice their opponents, as though they were too small to be seen. He nodded and said, 'He is about twenty, not a big man, but broad in the shoulder. He carries his left hand in his tunic, as though to protect it. He seems a thoughtful fellow; and good-looking, apart from his broken nose. I think he has lived among the Normans, for his yellow hair is cropped as short as a sheep's back.'

Kormac said, 'He doesn't fight with his hair. It is that left hand I am interested in. I never liked fighting left-handed men; they come in on the wrong side. But we'll manage, friend. I'll make him change hands early on, then he'll be at a disadvantage. Are there any priests with him?'

The man shook his head. Kormac smiled and said, 'Thank God for that! It's bad enough fighting against a queen's champion, without fighting the Pope as well.'

The Englishman walked up from the boat, ahead of his velvet-cloaked companions, pulled hard on the hazel stakes, as though testing them, then stared at the sun, as if he were deciding where he should stand in the combat.

All the time he was whistling between his teeth, almost sound-lessly, like a groom rubbing down a horse. It was a monotonous little tune, and seemed to annoy the courtiers, who stood in a small group on their own, away from Kormac's followers.

The Englishman stripped off his short byrnie, his tunic, and undershirt, flinging them carelessly beyond the holmgang-field. Kormac's men watched him keenly. His body was lean and white, as though it had not seen much sun. But his muscles, though youthful, were those of a lithe, fast-moving man. In the middle of his chest was tattooed a small serpent coiling round a cross.

The grey-haired man whispered to Kormac, who did not bother to turn round, but said, 'My sword, Lang, will chop its tail off! It won't wriggle then.'

The Englishman must have heard this, but he went on whist-ling. Then he scratched his cropped head violently, as though it itched; and after that he stooped and drew his sword from its long, clumsy-looking sheepskin sheath.

The sword was also long, but it was not clumsy. Its blade was narrower than most men had seen, and was polished as brightly as silver. Down its middle ran an intertwining pattern in blue steel, and its bronze cross-pieces were curved downwards and shaped like lions drinking. Its pommel was of black jet that glinted like a jewel in the sun, but not prettily.

The Englishman began to sing in a hoarse voice:

> *Nadr, Serpent of the Wound,*
> *Dinner is almost ready.*
> *Are your teeth sharp, Nadr?*
> *Are you thirsty, then?*
> *Do not fret, little one,*
> *All will soon be yours.*

Then, without warning, he began to whirl the sword round his head, so fast that it seemed like a blinding circle of light. The sound it made was that of a snake hissing.

The man with grey hair whispered, 'I do not like this, Kormac.'

Kormac reached down and took another drink from his beer-horn, then, wiping his lips, said, 'Just a young cock crowing to keep his courage up.'

'His left arm, from knuckle to shoulder, is covered with old scars.'

'I've got as many myself—aye, and down my body, too, to the waist.'

The grey-haired man said, 'He has no scars on his body. That speaks of nimble legs, Kormac.'

The men were ready, and a tall fellow called Hrut began to cry out the rules of holmgang; that each man was entitled to wear out three shields, held before him by a chosen follower; that if his sword got broken, he could use axe or dagger; that once blood flowed on to the skins in the middle, the fight was to stop; that if either man was driven back beyond the hazel stakes he should be declared *nithing*, and unworthy of manhood.

Kormac had heard these words a hundred times and did not listen. The Englishman nodded at each rule, then went on whistling and smiling in a pleasant way.

When Hrut called out and asked them to choose their shield-holders, both men shook their heads and waited for the signal to start. Hrut gave it and the combat began.

At first they circled each other like wary dogs, watching keenly, trying to gain the advantage of the sun. Then suddenly Kormac's sword streaked out. Men held their breath. The Englishman swayed sideways, lifted his arm, and let the blade pass harmlessly. Before the giant could draw it back, he had been hit across the top of his head with the flat of Nadr.

Kormac did not cry out, though the blow sounded like a man chopping wood for kindling. But his eyes blurred and his face wrinkled up and became very red.

The Englishman did not press home his advantage, but

stepped back a pace and sang, 'All will soon be yours, little one.' Kormac heard this and his anger flared. He rushed forward and swept Lang outwards like a mower's scythe. The Englishman had to give ground, until his back was set against one of the hazel stakes.

Kormac's followers sucked in their breath, sure that the Englishman would be defeated now. Then they saw why he had dragged on the hazel poles earlier, testing them. For he was leaning against one of them, almost like a man sitting on a bench, and parrying Kormac's blows with easy movements.

'It is like an old woman spinning,' shouted a Northman called Ubbi. 'Come away from the stake and fight, Saxon.'

The Englishman spoke for the first time and said, 'Go home and milk your goats, comrade.'

He could not have chosen more telling words, for Ubbi had seven goats and was always talking about them. The crowd laughed, already liking the young man. But the black-clothed courtiers frowned, as though they did not care for such unknightly comments.

It would have been better if everyone had stayed silent, for while that gust of laughter blew, Kormac swept in and struck the Englishman a blow on the point of the left shoulder, as he had said he would do. The bright sword dropped from the youth's hand on to the turf. Then he stood unarmed, rubbing his shoulder and looking at his arm. There was no blood on it, because Kormac's sword had twisted in his grip and only the flat of the blade had struck.

For a second Kormac made as though he was getting into position to give the death-blow; but the Englishman did not even look at him. Instead, he kept rubbing his shoulder, and gazing beyond the alder trees as though he thought of going down to the river to fish.

Kormac lowered his sword and said abruptly, 'We can't end it so soon. Men would say I fought a mere boy. I declare a rest-space.'

He turned and walked back to the grey-haired man. The

Englishman bent and picked up his sword in his right hand, shaking it again, ignoring the courtiers, most of whom were frowning at him as though he was their enemy and not their champion.

Kormac called over, 'If you are thirsty, there is beer enough for two in this horn, boy.'

The Englishman shook his cropped head and said, 'Later, thank you. Then I can drink it all.'

Once more the crowd laughed. Kormac was furious. He rose to his feet and clenched his hand about his sword.

'Come, then,' he said, 'you shall have your drink in heaven with the angels!'

But the Englishman held up his hand to halt him for a moment while he went over to the skin in the centre, and tried to smooth out a fold with his foot. Then, finding it impossible, he shrugged and turned to face Kormac, the ruckled skin only a yard behind him. Kormac had noticed this, too, and smiled. It was such a fold that a shuffling man might trip over.

So when the fight began again, he flailed Lang so fiercely that no man could have stood against that sword. The Englishman moved back, his feet on the skin. Then, as everyone had expected, his heels struck the fold, he seemed to lose his balance, and he fell. Kormac's men were silent now, wondering how the kill would be made. The courtiers let out a snort of annoyance.

Kormac brought Lang down swiftly. But the Englishman, lying on the skin, simply moved his head and the bright-pointed blade buried itself nine inches in the ground.

Then, even as Kormac strained to pull it clear again, the youth on the skin took aim and smacked his own blade across the back of the giant's legs, just behind the knee. It was as though he was a boy whipping a top.

Kormac's face suddenly changed to a mask of agony. His big eyes went even bigger; his mouth opened, but no sound came out. Then his great hand unclasped and his sword dropped to the ground. He staggered, then fell like a ruined tower, his legs as useless as sticks.

The grey-haired man cried out, 'Look, the Englishman has ham-strung him! Kormac is finished!'

As men clustered round the fallen swordsman, the Englishman bent over him and said, 'Can you find a space in your groanings to declare that this was fair fight, comrade?'

Kormac wiped his hand over his face and said hoarsely, 'Yes, it was fair! Leave me.'

The Englishman said, 'Now will you declare that the Lady Gunhilda is a good woman, and not a wicked witch as you said before?'

Kormac was biting at the holmgang-skin, but he was able to nod and mutter, 'She is as you say. I was wrong.'

The Englishman patted him on the back and said, 'I am sorry it had to come to this. It was not of my choosing. I am her champion and earn my bread by obeying her. Now would you care to drink from your beer-horn? I will fetch it for you.'

Kormac gave a deep groan and shook his head. 'It is a priest I need, not a beer-horn. The beer is yours, leave me.'

The Englishman stood back so that Kormac's friends could get to him. Then he wiped his sword and put it away in the sheep-skin, and walked over to where Kormac had left the beer-horn. While he was drinking from it the boy, Egil, rushed up weeping and knocked the horn out of his hands.

Trembling with anger, he said, 'Kormac was worth three of you.'

The Englishman nodded and answered, 'Perhaps he was. But he lies on the ground now. If you wish to help him, then get your father to give him a job on his steading. Perhaps the man's legs will knit and then he will be able to hobble after the geese.'

As Egil went back towards Kormac, one of the courtiers touched the Englishman on the shoulder and said coldly, 'Come, it is time to return to the palace and tell our mistress that her good name has been successfully defended.'

The Englishman bowed his cropped head, like a servant obeying a command. He stopped only to fling five coins on to the skin beside Kormac, then he walked down to the waiting boat. On the way over the river none of the courtiers spoke to him. They looked about them blankly, as though he did not exist. But he was whistling and did not seem to mind.

2. Baldwin of Flanders

EMPRESS GUNHILDA, sister of King Harthacnut of England, and wife of Henry, Emperor of Germany, sat in the darkening hall of Count Baldwin of Flanders. She was a sad-faced woman with a pale skin and a heavy jaw that made her look more like a man, although her robe of stiff silk from Spain, with its Moorish embroidery, was very dainty. And for a woman of her size her feet were neat in Arabian slippers, covered with pearls.

Baldwin of Flanders sat on a dais below her, near the oak king-post of the hall. It was carved with an interlacing pattern that ended in a dragon's head, like the prows that northern men still put on their longships. A craftsman from Wisby in Gotland had carved this kingpost in return for a year's bread and board.

Baldwin was a fat-faced man with small eyes like a pig. When master in his own palace he was merry and drunken and loud-voiced. But when the wife of the German Emperor visited him he seemed to shrink to half his size. Some of his courtiers whispered that this was because of his bad conscience; because he had plotted for months to rebel against the Emperor; or because he had given rough northern men trade-rights to sell slaves in Flanders, against the wish of the Pope. Some even said his bad conscience was due to the fact that he planned to ally himself with Magnus of Norway and invade England. But those who thought they really knew hinted that he was simply afraid the moment he set eyes on Gunhilda, who always had a few sullen young men with her from the old Danelaw in England, men prepared to put a knife into any man who displeased their mistress.

This day, as twilight came on, Baldwin was more than ever uneasy. Earlier in the day a messenger had come clattering into the courtyard with a great deal of noise and the blowing of horns. In any other circumstance this would not have mattered; but this particular man came from Magnus of Norway and flaunted his banner of the White Bear for anyone to see.

Baldwin was hoping that the Empress Gunhilda had not been looking out of the upper window, or that some servant had not run whispering the news to her, for she detested Magnus.

Gunhilda had seen the messenger. She missed little; and specially those things she was not intended to see. Now, Count Baldwin of Flanders shuffled in his broad oak chair, waiting.

Gunhilda spoke at last. 'Life is most strange, my lord. I, the daughter of King Cnut, the sister of King Harthacnut, the wife of the Emperor of Germany, and the mistress of more castles than I can call to mind, am troubled. How do you account for that?'

Count Baldwin began to bite his lip. He wondered whether a spy had overheard his conversation with the messenger of Magnus. That fool with the White Bear banner had been quite outspoken about his master's plot to capture Gunhilda and hold her in Norway, so as to force her husband's support in the fighting against Swein of Denmark.

Baldwin kicked out at a dog that was passing; but he was clumsy and missed the creature.

'Lady, this world is a sad, dark place. We carry our load along its rocky paths to find heaven.'

He was hoping he could turn the talk into other, less dangerous, channels.

Gunhilda laughed contemptuously. 'Don't talk like a hedge-priest, Baldwin. You do well enough. If my husband did not show a friendly interest in you, then either the French King or the Duke of Normandy would march into Flanders for meddling in their affairs.'

Baldwin forced a humble smile. 'Dear lady, how is that

possible? Your great brother, Harthacnut, King of England, would never allow it. He knows how well I have tried to act towards his family. He knows that I gave him, and your blessed mother, Emma, shelter here in Flanders when all the nobles stood against them. He knows that I defied Earl Godwine of Wessex for his sake and that Godwine has never forgiven me. Further, he knows that any Englishman in trouble is welcome at my court. Lady, Flanders is almost like another English county!'

Gunhilda arranged one of her heavy flaxen plaits and spoke coldly. 'He knows nothing of the sort, Baldwin. He died suddenly at a wedding feast three days ago. He was always a drunken fool at feasts, my brother. He was a fool anyway. Look at the taxes he levied on the English to keep his lazy sailors loyal. Look at the way he burned Worcester down when two of his tax-collectors were killed—and no more than they deserved! Why, my good father, Cnut, must be turning in his grave even now.'

Baldwin crossed himself. 'One should speak no ill of the dead, lady,' he mumbled. 'Your brother sits in heaven now—and the news weighs on my heart—so we should forget his faults. We all have faults, lady. Even you and I, perhaps.'

Gunhilda gave a deep chuckle. 'You talk like a mumbling old monk, teaching the beef-brained sons of peasants. "We all have faults," you say. Of course we have, but some of us have the sense to keep them secret, or to turn them into virtues. I have faults; I like power, for instance. But I try to give value for every alliance I make. I am not mean with my gifts, Baldwin. No one could accuse me of that.'

Baldwin bowed his head meekly and muttered something that might be taken as praise. He did not dare look Gunhilda in the face—any more than he had ever dared look old King Cnut in the face. These Vikings were hard to talk to, he thought; they said such forthright things.

Gunhilda went on, almost to herself, 'But that fool of a brother—he was the tool of any earl who spoke fair words to him. Look how he fell in with Godwine, a man whose word can never be trusted once he has gone through the door! No man who drinks

14

as much as my brother should ever sit on a throne and conduct the affairs of a kingdom. Give Harthacnut four jugs of ale and he would sign an alliance with anyone who put a quill into his hand and helped him make his cross. Believe me, Baldwin, I do not sorrow for him. I sorrow for poor Edward, the one they already call "the Confessor". There's another fool, if you like—but a holy fool. He spends more time on his knees than on his feet, silly fellow! And the earls laugh at him behind their hands. He is a pigeon ripe for the plucking, they think. And, be assured, they will pluck him before too long. He has spent too much of his time in Normandy to understand English ways. Before you can say a Mass, Saxon Godwine will have him married off to one of his daughters, and then there will be an end to royal power in England.'

Count Baldwin rose from his chair and scratched at his thin sandy hair. 'Lady, lady, we should not speak of these great ones in this manner. Someone might hear.'

Gunhilda mocked him. 'Someone might hear! Why, have you another of your spies hidden behind the hangings, Count? Who should hear? And what does it matter if they do? I tell you, Edward is nearly forty, and he's as great a ninny as he was when he was four. I know him, don't forget. He is my half-brother. I used to play with him when we were children. I know what he is like—a prayer-gabbling milksop who should have been a priest. Why, Earl Godwine will mould him like clay once he gets his big butcher's hands on him. Mark my words.'

Baldwin was standing by the window, looking down into the courtyard. He knew that everything this loud-voiced queen said was true. He knew that her brother and her half-brother were fools; but he knew just as well that his place was to tolerate them all—the fools and the tyrants, the kings and the earls. Do them all a favour in turn—and so keep Flanders safe.

Just now he hoped to arrange matters so that Gunhilda made a journey into the north; then it would be the task of Magnus of Norway to keep her there. Once Gunhilda was locked up in Bergen, say, Baldwin might breathe freely again and have a little time to decide what to do next.

15

'Lady, to live one's life in these difficult times is much like doing a piece of embroidery. There are so many threads of so many colours, and they keep getting tangled.'

Gunhilda tapped with her long finger-nails on the arm of her chair. 'I think you are as big a fool as any of them, Baldwin. You are as crafty and drunken and priest-ridden as any man outside Rome, I swear. And always wondering whom you can betray next. Come now, don't look coy; you know I speak the truth.'

Baldwin was lost for words. In his mind he already pictured Gunhilda dressed in rags and lying on the straw in a northern dungeon. The thought pleased him. But the Empress's next words did not.

'I know you well enough, Count,' she said, smiling like an over-fed cat. 'I know that it was you and Magnus of Norway who put about the rumour that I was a witch. I have my own spies, you see. And they speak the truth—not like those under-paid rogues you keep in your own kitchens! I have my champions, too, my lord. That young Englishman who is out fighting the rogue Kormac for me now at Holmganga is one of many. He would cut your throat before you could take a fresh breath if I but snapped my fingers—so!'

She snapped her fingers, and Baldwin shuddered. He put his hand up to his twitching mouth. 'Lady, let us jest no further. As for the poor boy you mention, he may be lying stark on Holmganga this very moment. We should say a prayer for him, not joke as we are doing.'

The heavy oak door suddenly swung open and the Englishman stood there, smiling. In his battered mail and with his long sword hanging down in its sheepskin scabbard by his leg, he looked more like a brigand of the heathland than a courtier.

He looked down at Baldwin and said, 'I need no prayers, Count. Keep them for Kormac, the killer someone sent to finish me. The killer who will kill no more—unless he learns to fight from a stool.'

He paced into the room and Gunhilda smiled at him, as an indulgent mother would smile at a too-forward son whom she doted on.

'So, my good name is safe?' she said.

The young man answered, 'I have crippled Kormac, lady. That is all I know.'

'Hereward, I am the luckiest woman in Europe to have such a champion as you.'

The Englishman said in his light voice, 'That's as may be, lady. I come to claim my reward.'

For an instant even Gunhilda was taken aback. But then she smiled again. 'Yes, my young eagle. I promised you your heart's desire. What is it? Name it and you shall have it.'

Hereward walked over to the hearth-fire in the middle of the hall and kicked at the smouldering embers. With his back to the Empress, he said firmly, 'I hear great things of your kinsman, Swein of Denmark. I would like to visit him and see what pickings there are to be had in the north. Swein would pay well for another sword to help him against Magnus, would he not, lady?'

Gunhilda pursed her lips for a moment, then smiled. 'I will give you the best harness and weapons, the best horse—all a warrior could want. And, what is more, I will make the journey north myself, with you as my protector. My husband is too busy about his own affairs—quarrelling with popes and princes—to mind what I do. And I could take you to Swein. He will listen to me, Hereward. I will see that he gives you an army to lead, never fear.'

Hereward knelt down by the dog and began to pull its ears, trying to make it bite him. But the dog was old and good-natured. It liked the scent of this Englishman, and the rough way he played. The dog began to lick the swordsman's face until Hereward pushed it away, laughing.

'I do not want an army,' he said. 'I want armour, weapons, a horse, a ship, perhaps—and the chance to make a fortune.'

Gunhilda smiled and shook her head. 'You can never forget your father was only a thegn, can you?'

Hereward's face was grim for an instant. 'I can never forget that my mother was a Dane,' he said. 'And that we held lands and houses—until your brother, Harthacnut, burned us out for killing tax-collectors we had never even seen.'

Baldwin drew in his breath and was about to say that such talk was treason. But Gunhilda only nodded.

'Yes, my brother was a fool to ill-treat folk like yours. But he is dead now, and I shall make amends. Never fear, Gunhilda rewards her friends—and punishes her enemies.'

She gave Baldwin a sly look as the young man escorted her from the room.

The Count bowed his head. But in his heart there was no humbleness. He was wondering where it would be best for his men to ambush Gunhilda and her arrogant young champion as they travelled north to Denmark. Magnus of Norway would pay a high price for two such birds, he suddenly decided. They would make good hostages.

3. Visitors from England

KING SWEIN of Denmark, nephew of old King Cnut and cousin of the Empress Gunhilda, was sitting in his hall at Aarhus eating figs. Each year, just before the fall of the leaf, a Russian trader would come to Aarhus with a cargo of figs wrapped in oiled silk for Swein. On the silk wrapper were painted words in long flowing

Arabic script, which Swein used to love tracing with his finger. The trader told him that the Arabic was a magic spell to bring him good fortune and was written by a Saracen wizard. No one at Swein's court knew Arabic—and scarcely any Latin—so the trader's word was never questioned.

King Swein made one of his craftsmen carve the Arabic shapes into the interlacing pattern of his kingpost, down the back of his oak chair, across the face of his coffer chest where he kept his fur robes; and he even had his swordsmith inlay the inscription in silver plate down the middle of his sword-blade. This sword was called Blood-torch and had a pommel as big as a crab-apple of jet from Whitby in England. Swein wanted it to be a better sword than that of King Magnus, which was called Leg-biter and had guards of walrus tusk and a hilt covered with beaten gold. In everything Swein wished to become the better of Magnus, though this did not often happen. All the same, Blood-torch had great luck. The first time he carried it Swein killed three wolves and a German baron who would not let the royal hunting-party pass through a narrow stone gate. So Swein had great faith in the Arabic spell, and even said that one day it would regain him the kingdom of Norway. When he told the Russian trader about this the man said, 'Lord, you have wisdom. The power of that spell is great—but just as great is the power of the figs. They are a magic fruit—as you can see, they are like nothing else—but must be eaten regularly, just as one must pray regularly if good is to come from it. Am I to increase the amount next year?'

King Swein nodded. Next year the price of the figs doubled, because, as the Russian said, magic was harder to come by in the East since so many Norman war-bands were passing through the countryside and carrying Christianity there.

But Swein paid without complaint and had special iron coffers made with treble locks so that no one else should steal his figs and gain power. He did not even offer them to ambassadors from England—although he was well thought of in that country, where his uncle had once been King, and his cousin, Harthacnut, the King after him.

On this day Swein had three visitors from England. He did not wish to receive them with his mouth full—nor did he wish to share his fruit, as a good host should on such occasions.

The Englishmen were outside, waiting in the little dark anteroom. Swein could hear them coughing and clanking their long swords against the benches and swearing at the dogs.

He swallowed the last fig and beat on the floor with his council-staff for the door to be opened.

The Englishmen entered, looking very black of brow and tight of lip at having been kept waiting. The first one was a head taller than Swein, wore a ragged cloak, and had an untrimmed beard. The mail armour under his rough wool tunic was red with rust. But his heavy sword was contained in a polished black leather scabbard tipped with a chape of gold. The Englishman held this sword as though it were a great kingdom, and when he bowed before Swein he was concerned not to let the gold chape knock against the table-leg.

Swein put his arms about the Englishman's neck and embraced him. 'Why, God be praised,' he said, 'you have arrived safely, Earl Godwine. The seas have been rough, my shipmen tell me. Even they have had to neglect the silver fish and eat mutton. Yet you pass over the waves with only rust on your mail to show for it.'

Earl Godwine made a pretence at a smile and then sat down on an oak bench without being invited. He said in a rough mumbling voice, 'Swein Estrithson, the seas were bad; but if they had topped my mainmast, I still must have come. Yes, even if I had had to walk on the sea-bottom.'

Swein smiled and nodded. This was the way Godwine always spoke—as though he had power over wind and wave and thunder, as well as over the English earls and the new English King, Edward.

'You would not surprise me, whatever you did,' he answered, wondering what the Englishman was going to say.

Earl Godwine cleared his throat and pointed to one of the others, a man with a pointed red beard already well grown. 'This is my son, my eldest, named Swein like yourself. He's a fool, my friend, but a good man with the horse and the sword. Can you give him house-room?'

King Swein nodded, wondering why Godwine should be so anxious to send one of his sons away. Godwine answered this question in his next breath.

'This madman has tried to marry an abbess—of all things to do—and now the bishops are yelping after his excommunication. He could have chosen any woman in England—but he has to pick a woman who has vowed herself to God! Not even the King can save him—if indeed our new King wants to. It is my belief that Edward is glad that such ill fame has come to my family, praying dotard that he is!'

King Swein pulled at his lip and said, 'All young fellows make mistakes. I married five times before I found the woman I could truly love. That is not important. What of your son's earldom— now that *is* important.'

Godwine thumped the table hard and said, 'He has lost that, the young ass. The court is full of Normans now—barons and bishops and so on. They will not hear of him staying a minute longer on English soil. They treat him like a wolf. A son of mine— like a flea-bitten wolf.'

Earl Swein began to shuffle on the stone floor and to look angry. 'All will be well, father,' he said. 'When my sister has had a chance to plead for me. She *is* the Queen of England.'

Godwine blew out his breath with a great sound and clenched hard on his sword-hilt. 'Before God,' he swore, 'was there ever a man blighted by such an idiot of a son! Don't you understand, fool, that your sister cannot overrule bishops? And if she could, she is powerless against barons. But Holy Edward will never listen to her. He is in the hand of the Church.'

King Swein rubbed his long nose. 'Perhaps you have the answer there, Earl Godwine. If your son made the pilgrimage to Jerusalem . . .'

But King Swein got no further. The third Englishman stepped forward and even leaned on the King's chair. His face was very flat and very hard, covered with crossed sword-cuts and tufts of

21

dark beard growing right up to his eyes. His fingernails were ridged and ragged. He had two daggers in his belt.

He said, 'I am Harold, King.'

King Swein drew away a little, wondering if this Harold was the berserk that men said. His voice was very rough, more used to shouting than talking, it seemed. The Danish King smiled and said, 'I knew who you were, Earl. I saw the great ring of Wessex on your finger. I am fortunate to greet such a warrior. They say over here that you make a practice of killing five Welshmen before breakfast. Is that true?'

Harold Godwinson did not smile at this remark. His eyes were flat and grey and empty-looking. He stared through Swein as though he was reading the Arabic inscription on the back of the oak chair. He said, 'Welshmen are great fighters, King. I have killed a few—but only by luck. The oldest of the gods fight on their side. It is not of Welshmen I will speak. I speak of my brother, Earl Swein. We are a great family. We hold three parts of England. We have a sister for Queen. And before we have done, we may be even greater. This I tell you so that you will understand. Things will change in England, Swein Estrithson. The Normans think that they are already masters there, but the Godwine family will show them that the old days can still come back. A man of Danish blood can still sit on the throne in Winchester.'

King Swein's eyes gleamed for a moment. He thought that Harold was speaking of him. But it was not so.

'I am brother to the Queen,' Harold went on flatly. 'And my mother was sister to King Cnut. One day, who knows, the gods may throw the crown into my lap.'

King Swein looked up almost in horror, but Harold's face was still set and expressionless. Earl Godwine was playing with a small meat-knife that a servant had left on the trestle-table and smiling.

King Swein forced a smile to his own lips and said, 'Yes, Earl Harold; what then?'

Harold loosed his hold on the arm of the King's chair and went back to Earl Swein, putting his arm about him and standing firm.

'This,' he said. 'I will not have any brother of mine packed off to Jerusalem like a common rogue to make his peace with the Church. I want him to stay here, where he can be called upon if the need rises, not shrivelling away in some desert place and leaving his bones for jackals.'

King Swein folded his hands in his lap and said, 'I think it can be arranged, lords. There is nothing strange in what you ask. After all, my own brother Beorn has an earldom in England, and my other brother, Osbern, leads a comfortable life there, too. Perhaps one day he may become an earl as well.'

Godwine was digging the little knife into the table and did not answer. So the King said hastily, 'It shall be as you say; Earl Swein shall stay here and be treated like my own son. How does that seem to you all?'

Only Earl Godwine answered quietly, looking down at the point of the knife. 'It is as well. You will get our support when you fight against Magnus of Norway. We shall also support the Emperor, and my daughter will see that our King Edward does the same. So you will end by having us all on your side against Magnus. Is that not a good bargain?'

King Swein hesitated. To have *Englishmen* telling him what to do—and men who were not even kings! They were hardly more than brigands, though of noble blood. They had not been into the dark groves at midnight to wash in the blood of the sacred horse; they had not dreamed the 'King's Dream', when Odin came to the dreamer like a raven and spoke the words of blessing; nor had they then gone to church and been anointed by the bishops and given a cross of sticks to carry before all the people.

All the same, thought King Swein, a man must do as he may. He bowed his head to Earl Godwine and said, 'I will protect your son. And I will join you in putting an end to Count Baldwin. In return, I call on the unseen witnesses to hear that you have promised to help me in destroying Magnus of Norway.'

He expected Godwine and his sons to get on their knees to him then, but they were hardly listening. They were looking at something that was happening outside in the courtyard.

23

Annoyed, King Swein got up from his chair and said, 'What is it?'

Godwine flung the knife carelessly into a corner and yawned. 'There is a woman, carried in a litter. She has fifty knights with her. They carry the banner of the German Emperor, so it must be Gunhilda who comes.'

Earl Swein laughed and said, 'Why, that old nag! She must be coming to ask for another young man to protect her. Her great husband, the Emperor, seems to neglect her—and I don't wonder! They say that any young Englishman with a good sword arm can get service in her retinue. I even thought of going myself!'

Earl Harold's lips tightened and his beard jutted out. For a moment it seemed that he might strike his brother. But instead he said grimly, 'You forget who you are, brother. Save yourself for better things. From what I can see through the window, she has a champion already. A crop-haired English-looking fellow with a broken byrnie. He'll be some adventurer with an empty belly and a thirsty sword, no doubt.'

King Swein looked into the courtyard.

'The young man's name is Hereward,' he said. 'He came over to defend the Empress's good name in Flanders against one of the berserks that Magnus sends about the countryside. A giant called Kormac.'

Earl Godwine turned from the window and snorted. 'I have heard of this Hereward,' he said. 'His father was a small thegn in the Fenland. He got burned out when that fool Harthacnut went mad and thought he had a rebellion to deal with. Hereward is nothing but a young sword-swinger. If Gunhilda depends on him, then the world has grown to be a playground for idiots and children.'

Earl Harold was sitting in King Swein's chair now, tugging at his tufted beard. 'I have been thinking, father,' he said, 'that what my brother suggested was not so stupid, after all. Suppose one of us did become her champion, by killing this Hereward if needs be, then would not the German Emperor think the more highly of us? Hereward will have no family to pay blood-money to; and no one

24

need know anything of the affair. It would ill become a son of Godwine to neglect such a chance as this to put himself in favour.'

Godwine began to laugh. 'Please yourselves, my sons,' he said. 'You have never waited for my advice before—and it is late to start now. Kill Hereward if you wish, but first see that he is not too great a favourite with Gunhilda. If his death offended her, then she would turn her husband against us—and, like King Swein here, we need the Emperor's good will at this moment.'

King Swein was biting at his beard and twisting his fingers till the knuckles cracked. These Godwines always brought trouble! They were a plague on the peace of the world. He wished he had never promised friendship to them.

Like a frightened hare when the dogs surround it, he turned one way and then another. At last he said, 'For the love of God, lords, be discreet. Be sensible. And if you must kill him, then let it not happen in my house. I want none of his blood on my hearthstone. Do it somewhere away, out in the fields perhaps—but not here. If it offended the Empress, then she might side with Magnus. Take care, I beg you.'

Earl Swein patted the King of Denmark on the shoulder. 'Courage, cousin, courage!' he said, sneering. 'A man must be willing to face the whole world—and the heavens, too—or he is no man.'

4. King Swein's Figs

GUNHILDA CAME in like a Valkyrie, her eyes blazing in her white face. Even her pale hair had fallen from its net and seemed to flame on her broad shoulders. King Swein was about to kneel before her out of courtesy, but she grasped the neck of his shirt and almost pulled him upright.

'Christendom in flames!' she said in a loud voice. 'But I was shot at after I had come over your march. Look at this hole in my skirt! Look at this tear in my bodice! Is this the way to greet a guest? Is it? Look you, Danishman, it is one thing for a woman to be molested in Flanders—but here I expect to be treated like the wife of your nearest neighbour, the Emperor. I expect . . .'

King Swein was backing away from her anger, speechless. But Earl Godwine let out a great laugh and slapped Gunhilda on the shoulder, as though he was greeting another man.

'Harthacnut's sister!' he roared. 'Well, by the Rood, but your temper hasn't mended a bit since you nearly scratched my eye out for stealing a kiss that Michaelmas!'

Gunhilda turned on him, in the dark room, her head forward as though she would bite him. When she saw who it was she made her hand into a fist, as though she would punch him. But Earl Godwine began to shake her hand up and down.

Bewildered, Gunhilda said, 'What devilry are you plotting up here in Denmark? We thought there was one place in the north where we could talk in peace without having a Godwine in the room!'

The Earl smiled grimly at the insult, but only said, 'Two of my sons are in Normandy, and another is thinking to visit Jerusalem. If Harold here can spare the time next spring, I would like him to go down to Miklagard—I forget, you call it Constantinople, don't you?—and make friends with whatever emperor they have there now. So, soon you'll have to go to Iceland if you want to avoid your cousins, Gunhilda!'

King Swein broke into the talk now and said, 'When I go to Iceland it will be with a sword.'

Godwine nodded towards him, smiling, and said pleasantly to Gunhilda, 'He is still bearing malice, you see. Those Icelander earls have sided with Magnus, but they will come back to you fast enough if we show them Magnus's head on a pole. That would be a better persuader than any clerkly words!'

A young man who had followed Gunhilda and stood in the shadows suddenly said, 'Give the word, lady, and I will bring you that head—and a pole to set it on.'

26

All was silent then in the King's room. They could hear the fire lapping at the spruce logs on the hearth. Godwine turned and saw Hereward leaning at the lintel, his thumbs in his belt and his big sword hanging before him between his legs.

Earl Godwine said, 'Since when must lords halt in their talk while a peasant's son passes an opinion?'

Hereward pretended to pick something from his teeth, then made the motion of spitting, very gently, in the Earl's direction.

King Swein gasped with astonishment. Even Gunhilda drew her breath in. 'Hereward . . .' she began.

But Earl Harold took three paces across the room and stood before Hereward, face to face, glowering. They were of the same height and the same age, within a month or two. They could have been brothers but for the colour of their hair and the difference in their dress.

Hereward looked back lazily into Harold's eyes and said, 'Godwinson, well met! They told me you were a fighting-cock. Shake hands with another Northman.'

Hereward held out his hand quietly, gently, almost as though he knew Harold would not take it. Harold saw this; he also saw that this hand was so placed that it could draw the sword just as easily. It was then that he first realized what manner of man the Empress had chosen to protect her.

He stepped back a pace and looked under his dark brow at the Englishman. He drew in a deep breath and said quietly, 'Anywhere you like, but not here. No blood on King Swein's hearth-stone— that is the law. But anywhere outside his wall—and with sword or axe.'

Hereward put his hands behind his back now, to show that he was not afraid of Harold Godwinson. Then he said for all to hear, 'I meant no disrespect to you and yours. But I am a carle in the house of the Empress and so I have a right to be next to her and to speak for her. That is my duty and my privilege. Not even Godwine and his brave sons can take that right from me. As for fighting you, Harold Godwinson, I would not do that in the house

27

of King Swein; but, have no doubt, I would do it anywhere else, if my lady wished it.'

Gunhilda strode across the stone floor and stood between the young men. She put a hand on the shoulder of each and said, 'It is a sin against manhood for two such young bulls as you to spoil each other. The world is too short of brave ones for such fighters to spill each other's blood, even if one of them is a Godwine.'

Earl Godwine laughed again, but more grimly this time, and said, 'Let them be, Gunhilda. Young men will always be testing one another. It is a natural law we cannot break. Sooner or later these two will be at each other, by day or by night, to prove who has the stronger arm, the quicker eye. They both wish to be heroes, and who are we to stop them? This is beyond kings and queens and priests. It is beyond kingdoms and churches and such prattle. They are both Vikings, Gunhilda, and they will fight it out, one way or another, whatever you say.'

Gunhilda let her hands fall and stood back, her broad face white with fury. Her very mouth was pale, and her bosom rose and fell as though she was panting after swimming across a river. She said coldly, 'Earl Godwine, I love Hereward like my own son. I plan great things for him—lands, perhaps a crown. I set him as high as any Norman duke, as high as any English earl. Remember that. And remember, too, that my husband who is an emperor and speaks with popes as their equal will love Hereward just as I do. Let your son think of that before he goes seeking quarrels for himself. And let him recall also that this time he may have picked up a viper—not a stingless Welsh grass-snake!'

When she said this Earl Harold began to tear at his gold neck-ring, as though he was choking. His face went very red and spittle began to run out of his mouth-corners. All his limbs started to shake like those of an old beggar with the palsy. His brother, Swein, ran to him and began to speak softly, but Harold shook him off and began to cry out, using howls not words. King Swein knew the signs of berserk madness well enough and went to the door to call out for a leech to come and give Harold a potion to quieten him.

But Earl Godwine suddenly eased himself up from the oak trestle-table and struck his son across the side of the head with the back of his hand.

'Down, you mad dog!' he cried. 'Control yourself! Is this the time? Are you a girl, to cry for what you can't have?'

Once again he slapped Harold across the face, while King Swein clutched, white-knuckled, at the dragon-head of his chair, wondering why he of all men should have to tolerate such scenes in his own house.

Gunhilda stood so close to Hereward that any sweep of the sword would now strike her also. And still Hereward's hands were behind his back as he leaned, smiling, against the carved doorposts.

Harold Godwinson sank down to his knees suddenly and with his gnarled hands over his face began to weep. The tears ran out between his fingers, over the great ugly ring of Wessex, and on to the grey stone floor. If any other man had done this it would have been laughable. But with Harold it was a terrible sight to see. For a moment King Swein thought that there was magic about, for the tears looked like drops of blood to him. But it was only that Harold's hands were dirty with the red earth he had ridden through to reach Aarhus. And soon the tears were clear again and not red.

Gunhilda whispered to Hereward, 'In God's name, boy, leave this room. Go down to the other carles and keep out of the way of the Godwines. You only cause trouble.'

Hereward was about to make a reply, still smiling; but the Empress touched him on the chest and said, 'I command it. You know who I am.' The smile froze on Hereward's face and he bowed before her and left the room.

When he had gone Gunhilda quietened Harold, telling him roundly it was wrong to quarrel in another man's house. At last Harold seemed to see sense, and, in his abrupt way, begged the Danish King's pardon.

King Swein was weary of them all. He went to his fig-chest and unlocked it.

'Here,' he said, 'taste this fruit. This will put all unwise thoughts out of your heads.'

He began to chew at the plumpest fig he could find, feeling the magic coming into him with each bite. Gunhilda, who had had figs before, wasted no time in eating as many as she could. But Earl Godwine went to the window and stared out, ignoring the fruit. This hurt King Swein, but not so much as the thing Earl Swein was doing. He took a handful of figs, then, having tasted each one, spat out the fruit and flung the precious pieces into the fire.

'This is Eastern rubbish!' he said. 'Soon we shall all fall sick of the plague from eating such things. I tell you, King of Denmark, this is some Saracen plot. These things are not fruits, they are mummified parts of dead men, Christians, most like. If you are wise, you will get the bishop to shrive you before the sickness gets a hold on you!'

King Swein began to wonder. Perhaps young Godwine was right. There *was* something strange about figs; they were not like apples or pears. He began to trace the Arabic carving on his chair with his finger, as a protection. Then he suddenly thought that this would not do either. Perhaps the Arabic meant something bad, something evil against him, too. And he would only be quickening his doom by tracing it. He wished that the Godwines had stayed away from his house. He even wished that Gunhilda would go back to her husband in Germany, and take that young carle Hereward with her.

'Tomorrow,' he thought, 'I will get the Bishop from Odense to wash me with holy water. It is lucky he is staying in Aarhus now. And if he cannot promise me complete freedom from plague, then we will see what *his* head looks like on a spike. I pay my dues to the Church—I will have value for them, or know why.'

But the next day something happened which caused King Swein to forget all about the Bishop, or even the plague. He forgot about them both so effectively that before midday he had eaten half his store of figs in his anxiety, without a thought of Saracen magic any more.

5. Attack at Night

JUST BEFORE the bell of Aarhus Kirk rang for Prime, when the sun came flaring across the Sound like a barn-fire, there was a great shouting in the courtyard.

Kitchen-women ran about yelling and covering their heads with shawls, and all the dogs started to bark so wildly that the hawks in the mews jumped up and down on their perches like mad things.

King Swein was already awake. He ran to the nearest window and looked down.

Two shag-haired thralls were carrying a limp bundle wrapped in old blankets. They were finding it very heavy and were telling all who would listen that if they had been free men they would have left the body where they found it, lying in a ditch. But, they said, it was the body of a carle, and so they had to bring it in, though there was little enough life left in the man.

King Swein, who was responsible for paying blood-debts to the families of any of his carles who got hurt in his service, felt that life was using him unfairly these last days. He put on a gown of thick wool and went downstairs.

Gunhilda was already before him, her hair hanging wild down her back. She was out in the yard, kneeling over the body and cursing the Godwines.

Over her shoulder, King Swein saw that the wounded carle was Hereward, and not one of his own men. He was thankful for that, until the Empress turned on him and said, 'You dotard! So you give shelter to murderers here! Much good will that do you when my husband, the Emperor, hears of it. You listen to Godwine Snake-tongue, who promises you a rainbow—but you never stop

31

to think that my man can give you the sun and the moon if he so wishes. Well, you may look to see King Magnus coming down through the Skager Rak any month now—and with fifty ships from Germany beside him.'

She turned from Swein and went on stripping Hereward to find his wounds. There was a deep one in his back, under his left shoulder-blade. And another on his chest, just beneath his byrnie.

Swein felt angry and sick and weak and miserable and weary—all at the same time. Just because a carle, and an English carle at that, had been hurt in a fight, he must lose Denmark.

'Curse Earl Godwine!' he said to himself. 'And his two sons! May they burn!'

Gunhilda turned once more and said with venom like a snake, 'And as for your kinsmen, Beorn and Osbern, in England—well, you can look to see the burying of them within the week. My arm may be a woman's, but it is long.'

Swein mopped his wet face and turned to a Danish carle who had just appeared, rubbing the sleep from his eyes.

'Run to the guest-house,' he said. 'Bolt the doors and set a guard about it. Hold the Godwines, even if you have to put a spear into them. But tell the men not to do that unless it is very needful. Hurry, man, hurry!'

As the carle shambled away King Swein bent over Hereward. The Englishman had lost a deal of blood and his eyes were very dark and glazed. A cut on the head matted the cropped hair down one side, and he had bled from the ears. That was not a good sign, Swein thought. Usually it meant an injury to the brain.

Swein said to Gunhilda, 'I have sent men to hold Godwine. He is my kinsman, but I will punish him.'

The Empress was bathing Hereward's wounds gently and she did not turn. But she said, 'He is my kinsman, too. But this boy means more to me than any kinsman, Denmark.'

The King's leech came tut-tutting then and had Hereward carried into the hall. King Swein tried to think of his great father, Ulf of Norway, and of his brave hero grandfather, Swein Forkbeard, who had killed a dragon and burned thirty churches in his time. But no comfort came from them.

Nor did it come from the carle who rushed back to him. 'The guest-house is empty,' the man shouted. 'The beds were not slept in, Swein. A thrall told me he saw the three Godwines riding southwards like black demons two hours before dawn. There is no horse living that could catch them now.'

When King Swein struck him across the face, the carle did not complain. He had lived at Harthacnut's court at one time and knew that he was lucky to be treated so mildly, being the bearer of ill tidings.

King Swein met the leech on the stairs later. The old man shook his head and said, 'It is likely that he will live, lord. The wounds are deep, but we have put spider's webs over them and moss. The bleeding has stopped. He is young enough to heal well.'

Swein said, 'Then why, in God's name, do you wear this black face, man? Why does the mourning-harp sound in your voice, you old sheep?'

The leech shrugged his shoulders and said, 'We can mayhap heal the body—but what of the brain? That was the worst blow he took—and one he thinks that Harold gave him. He woke enough to tell us that—the three set on him as he came back from the village from seeing a girl he had taken a fancy to. The old Earl stuck him in the ribs, Swein came behind and put the dagger in his back. But he thinks it was Harold who hit him on the head when he was down and his helmet off. That was the coward's blow, and the direst.'

King Swein sat on a step, his face in his hands.

'Fetch the best leeches you can find,' he said. 'Fetch them up from Miklagard, from Syria, if you must. But see to it that this young fool gets well. Do that and I will give you your own weight in silver. I swear that before Odin and Christ.'

The leech rubbed his thin hand over his lips and said, 'We can heal the hole Swein's knife made. But it is my belief that Hereward will never be right in the head again.'

All the King said was, 'Heal the hole and be content. A berserk needs no brains!'

Later that day King Swein went to Gunhilda's chamber, where Hereward had been taken. All the window-holes had been covered with curtains to keep cold air away, and the room was heavy with the smell of potions and burning herbs. The leech was giving the carle a tincture of toad-flesh, dried and ground to powder, mixed in sour milk with the flesh of earthworms and spiders. As fast as he poured it down a horn funnel into Hereward's mouth, it ran out again, over his chest and on to the bedding. King Swein retched with the smell. 'Besides,' he thought, 'those sheets are of finest linen and are worth a cow, or three pigs. With this mess on them they will be ruined.'

He was going to say something about this, but Gunhilda was praying so fiercely at the bedside he did not dare.

Then, as he sat miserably, shuffling his feet and wishing he were anywhere—in Iceland or Ireland—the carle on the bed suddenly gave a great groan and sat up without warning. Gunhilda let out a little scream, the old leech dropped the horn funnel and the clay pot that held the filthy mixture. A serving-woman tried to push Hereward down again, but the carle swept out his heavy arm and knocked her sideways.

'Give me ale!' he shouted hoarsely. 'Give me ale! I have been at the oars all day and all night. Is this how King Swein treats a Viking? Where is the ale, I say? Have I brought a boatload of slaves from Northumbria for nothing?'

Queen Gunhilda stood up and reached out to comfort Hereward, but he even struck out at her and shouted, 'Take away this witch! This is the Saracen woman I told you about. Burn her at the stake, I warn you! Now bring me ale, and my sword. Ah, I see an old man here who tried to poison me. I will have *his* head first.'

Hereward began to struggle out of bed. The leech fell back afraid against the wall, his hand on his heart. Gunhilda ran weeping from the room to think her champion had lost his wits.

34

King Swein followed her, trying to tell her that one carle was not worth all this commotion.

He was half an hour consoling her, and when he crept up to the chamber again the room was empty. The fires had gone out. All that was left to tell the tale of that strange affair was a greasy mixture of the toad-potion on the fine linen sheets, mixed with blood, because the carle's wounds had opened again.

No one in the courtyard had seen Hereward pass, though one old woman, the widow of a thrall out on the lonely heathland, said that at twilight a troll with rolling eyes had come from a gorse-bush and had carried away a sheep. She had seen the troll begin to eat the creature raw, she said. First he ate the hind-legs, then the fore-legs, then the head. He was keeping the body for the last, she thought. When King Swein heard this he had the old woman whipped for lying. But he got no better truth out of her. Hereward was gone.

6. Boar's Head Helmet

LITTLE WONDER the questing carles of King Swein did not find Hereward. For ten days and nights he lay in the pigsty behind the old woman's house on the heathland, in a stone runnel covered with straw. She had seen him crawl there on hands and knees, moaning. But this was not the tale she had told King Swein. The King's men beat her quite hard, but the whipping was worth it, for she had gained a man in the house once more.

Yet for a while Hereward was little enough of a man. His body was thin and for almost a year the wounds in his chest and back gave him such pain that he could hardly lift a bucket, so that he had to walk bent like an old man. His hair had grown long in that time, and part of it, near his deep wound, had turned snow-white. He had lost both his sword and his byrnie, but this only troubled him vaguely, when he thought about it, which was not often.

The old widow-woman looked after him much better than the King's leech, using country remedies on his wounds—such herbal medicines as had been passed down the generations in a land where men had carried sword-hurts since the world's dawning-time.

And so, by one spring or another, she had got him right again—or as right as it seemed he would ever be. He and she would sit over the hearth-stone in the cold evenings, by the light of a tallow-fat rush, and talk. Once when carles broke in they took the couple for man and wife.

'What's your husband's name, old crone?' asked the captain.

Hereward had just enough sense to put on his thickest accent, such as the slaves and geburas of old King Cnut's time had used in Lincolnshire, and told them he was a Welshman called Griffog. When they asked him how he came to be in Denmark, he said that he had sailed in a curragh of tarred hide into the big sea to take service with Swein, but his flimsy boat had foundered on a skerry and a Danish ship had brought him into Lijmfiord.

The captain laughed loud and said, 'Thy heart seems good, Welshman, but Swein has no use for bent dry old tinder. He needs young stags to fight his battles. Still, even a good heart is worth something; so we will let you stay with this old hag here. Perhaps the store of this steading will increase with a man about, then King Swein will draw a bigger tithe from it. Fare you well, and watch that you don't burn the thatch down with your rushlights.'

When he had gone the old woman, Gytha, said, 'What does he expect us to do, sit in the dark?'

Hereward answered, 'I am always in the dark, candles or no. There is a darkness in my head that candles will not light.'

Gytha gave him warm goat-milk flavoured with wild honey and said, 'There, there, lad. It will be better next year, or the year after.'

To her, alone and friendless in the wind-blown land, one year was much like another, and had been so since her husband had an oak tree fall on him in a storm that blew right down from Iceland.

So King Swein never knew that Hereward was still in Denmark. As for Gunhilda, she soon forgot her young champion and found another, a Norman youth named Bertrand who could play the lute.

Strangely enough, Hereward's memory still recalled how a man should make hay, milk a cow or a goat, deliver a lamb, mend a thatch, and gather kindling. He did these things well enough, though for the space of three years he was very slow at everything—even at putting food into his mouth. But his memory did not yet recall sword-play, or anything to do with war. And for the time being the names of the Godwines had gone from him as though his mind was a parchment, scrubbed clean with sand so that something else could be written on it. He only knew, in his bad dreams, that there had been wicked men who had hurt him.

When he shouted out aloud in these dreams, old Gytha would comfort him. So he got to think of her as a mother, and when there was no one about even called her 'mother'. This pleased her, for she had never had children of her own.

Then, one winter five years or more after Hereward had first come to the lonely steading, he was in the barn sharpening an old axe to split kindling-wood. Outside, among the thick bushes, he suddenly heard a padding of feet and a harsh snuffling. He went to the door and saw pad-marks that seemed to go in a circle all about the sheep-pen. The marks were black in the white snow and you could not miss them.

Hereward pondered a while, then said to himself, 'That is a

wolf—and a big one. Wolves are the enemies of men. Master Wolf, you are my enemy!'

Hardly stopping to think what he was doing, he went from the barn to the place where the tracks ended. A big grey wolf lay among some holly bushes, snuffling and trying to bite at an arrow which stuck from his hind-leg. It had been there a long time, for he had bitten the feathers off it, and had gnawed the shaft far down. If the hair had not gone from his leg, it would have been hard to see.

Hereward stood near the wolf with the axe in his hand and said, 'You are an old wolf who cannot hunt with the others, so you come here to wait for the lambing season. You lie in ambush for the little beasts that cannot defend themselves, don't you, Master Wolf? And that is no fair fight, Master Wolf. You should know that a warrior must only fight his equals; and when he is wounded, he must give up all thought of being a warrior and must live in peace.'

While Hereward was talking the wolf stopped gnawing and licking and stared back at him with puzzled light eyes flecked with brown and amber. No man had ever talked to him before and Hereward wore a wolf-skin jacket that still carried the scent of its first possessor.

Then Hereward kneeled down close to the wolf and said, 'Here am I, at a disadvantage; just as you are. Now prove yourself, Master Lamb-killer.'

The wolf had got Hereward's true scent now and knew that he was a man, and a weak man at that. The creature shifted his hind-parts in the snow and sprang. To Hereward it was as though a cloak of darkness was being spread above him, and he struck upwards with the axe. Then the wolf fell down on to him, knocking him into the snow, yelping, and snapping at its own forefeet. Hereward got his breath back, rolled the animal from him, and used the axe again.

The wolf lay still. And while Hereward stood above it, watching for any sign of life, he heard the low sound of laughter behind him and turned round.

There was a man standing by a broken old stone wall, looking at him and nodding in a friendly fashion. He was a very big man, dressed in magnificent clothes. On his head was an iron helmet set with silver, clipping down under his jaws, a boar-head crest scowling from its peak. On his broad breast was battle-mesh of bronze and iron, every other link, and trimmed below in teeth. At neck and arm were gold bands. At waist, hand's breadth, was a war-belt spiked and studded with iron. His sword was almost the length of a man, his dagger half the width of that man's hand. His hair under his helmet down to his breast flared red as blood, its plait-ends wound with gold wire.

Such a man, his tall shield under his armpit, leaning, his legs crossed, his sword-tip in the snow, its pommel near his chin, his spear point rising like a pine-tree over his head, seemed a god.

Hereward gazed at him, wolf's blood over his body and face, and said at last, 'You, an old king come from under the ground, come from a howe?'

The man laughed again but only said, 'That was carle's axe-work, not thrall's. There were Vikings in the world when you first learned that stroke, man.'

Hereward tried to understand him, but the darkness got between the man's words and his understanding. He said, 'You, an old king then?'

The man shook his head. The gold wire tinkled on his shoulder-brooches. 'I am young yet,' he said. 'No old king. You are old. Perhaps fifty, perhaps sixty—but old. An old carle, young when Cnut was young, maybe. But old now.'

Hereward rose and wiped his hand across his brow. He felt old, true, but somehow he knew that he was not old. His hands were unwrinkled; his beard had not come to its full growth. He scratched his head, bewildered, and then said, 'I am trying to remember a man like you. There was a song I heard once, by a camp-fire in Germany. I forget how it went. It told of a man like you.'

The man eased his boar-head helmet up and said, 'Did it go like this?'

39

Then, in a high light voice he began to sing:

> *There was a man came from the north*
> *To Miklagard the grand;*
> *Like snow upon the wintry wind*
> *He blew across the land.*
>
> *He shook the city walls and rocked*
> *The tallest of the towers;*
> *But when the Emperor let him in*
> *He smiled—and there were flowers.*
>
> *Ten years he stayed in Miklagard*
> *And there was no more cold;*
> *Bees honey gave, and cows their milk,*
> *And all the streams ran gold.*
>
> *If he should leave the citadel*
> *The sky would fill with rain;*
> *And all the girls would lose their smiles,*
> *Winter would come again.*
>
> *'Varanger, stay with us,' they cry;*
> *'Don't leave us,' they all sing.*
> *'If you should go the sun would die;*
> *God would deny us spring.'*

He stopped singing and began to study his broad spade-shaped fingernails. Then he said, 'Was that the song, then?'

Hereward came to him, nodding, and said, 'Aye, that was the song. I only heard it a few times, but I have never forgotten it.'

There was a strange bird inlaid in silver on the man's round shield and about it spirals of copper, and curious signs like the tracks an adder leaves in the dust. Hereward bent over and traced the bird and the signs with his forefinger. The man let him do it, held out his shield a little so that he could reach. He said to Hereward, 'The bird is the raven, Landwaster. That is how the

Byzantines see him, with spiked wings. Such a bird could never fly, hey, grandad?'

Hereward shook his head. 'What are the others?' he asked. 'Are they old runes, then?'

The man said, 'That is the tongue of the Saracen. It is a prayer for luck in battle. An old emir I knew had that put on my shield for me. It calls on a god named Allah. He is like Jehovah or Odin—big and powerful in the air and the earth and under the sea. He is everywhere. If a man prays to him—as well as to Odin and the Whitechrist—then he can't go far wrong, can he, grandad?'

Hereward looked him steadily in the eye and said, 'If you call me that again, I shall take a foot off your height with this axe.'

The man said, 'Did you not hear about me in the song?'

Hereward waved his hand and said, 'That was a song. I am talking about "grandad". Stop it, or there will be no more songs; no more mouth to sing with.'

The man suddenly rested his shield by the wall and held out both his hands towards Hereward. 'Thank God,' he said. 'At last I have met a man who dares to threaten me—and to mean it! I have sailed and walked over half the world to find such a one. Now I find an old fellow in a greasy wolfskin with a rusty chopper in his hand who dares challenge me. God bless you, old brother.'

Hereward began to weep then, because he thought this man was a god, and he thought of himself as a worthless thing, hardly a man even.

Gytha came to the steading door and began to call out that Griffog the Welshman was sick and that no man worth his salt would fight with him.

But the warrior only smiled at her and said, 'Have no fear, old woman. This day I have found a real man. I tell you, it is easier to find gold, or a queen, or a stallion that can outrun the wind, than it is to find a man. He and I are the two men left in the world. He shall go with me and we will find a pair of thrones to sit on.'

Gytha sat down on the doorstep and began to wail with her shawl upon her head. Hereward went over to her and stroked her white hair gently.

'Do not mourn, mother. I will come back to you with gold. Be patient.' But Gytha only wept the more bitterly.

The big man came up behind him and said, 'My tongue trots ahead of my wit. Perhaps you should not leave your mother, after all.'

Hereward turned and said, 'If I stay here, I shall rot. Gytha has been good to me and one day I may return and bring something for her to make her happy. Let us go.'

The man frowned a little, then felt in his belt-purse and drew out a handful of gold coins. He laid them on the doorstep beside the old widow. Then the two turned and went through the snow. They looked back before they went over the hill and saw that Gytha still had her shawl over her head. The coins lay, faintly gleaming in the winter sun, beside her, untouched.

As they struck down towards the sea, the man said, 'Those were good gold bezants from Miklagard. A man could buy five horses with them.'

Hereward, who still carried the axe, halted and looked at the man. 'So you have bought me for the price of five horses,' he said suspiciously. 'You will make me your slave then?'

The man called back, 'Don't be a fool, Griffog. I have a hundred slaves, in Miklagard and in Kiev on the Russian river. I do not need you for that.'

Hereward said, 'That is as well. I may be slow in the wit, but today I have found my hand is still good on the axe-shaft. I have been a paid-man, I seem to remember—but I was never a slave.'

The big man waited for him and put his arm about his shoulders. 'Old Griffog,' he said, 'you are no slave now. You are my dear friend. I have known enough men, of white skin and brown skin and black skin, to know who is a true man and who a false. Be content now and give yourself to the great things that lie ahead.'

So the two stumbled on through the snow-drifts towards the sea, which lay two days ahead of them. The first night they stayed in a small village that had recently been visited by King Swein's carles, judging by the burned thatch here and there, and the lame men about in the fields and streets. Here, as they warmed their feet by a pine-log fire and drank mulled beer, they saw a strange thing through the window. A dog was sniffing along the muddy lane outside, when suddenly a cat appeared before it. The dog began to growl, as all dogs will, and the cat seemed about to give battle. But while the dog's attention was fixed on the cat, two other cats, one of them lacking a fore-leg, came from other directions and set on to him. There was snarling and barking and loud yowling, and the dog had the worst of it before he ran, helter-skelter, under a wood-pile for safety.

The big man laughed at this and said he always relished a good fight. But Hereward was dark-browed and grim. At last he said, 'That was like a dream which always troubles me—three against one; and two of them coming from behind. That happened to me, I think, once before the world grew sad about me.'

The man's smile left his broad face and he said gently, 'The old scar in your head, the wounds on your body. . . . Yes, I saw them when you took off the wolf-skin yesterday to wash in the stream. Three wounds may mean three men—with one like you who would not turn away from any man. Tell me, Griffog, who were the three men?'

Hereward tried to think, but always the truth slid away from his grasping and he shook his head.

The big man said, 'I can see by the white scars on your hands and arms that you have been in many battles. These three men must have come at you on some hill in Wales, when you and your clansmen held a shield-wall there against another chief. Is that it?'

Hereward shook his head again. 'They were not Welshmen,' he said. 'I cannot think what they were—but not Welshmen.'

The other drank deeply of his beer and said, 'Well, it matters not at all now, whether they were Welshmen, or Normans, or Englishmen.'

Hereward rose and kicked viciously at the logs on the fire. 'It still matters,' he answered. 'One day I will see them again, and then I will discuss a little matter with them. But the words will be spoken with an axe or a sword-edge.'

The man slapped him on the back and said, 'That is what I like to hear—good talk of vengeance! It is not what the Christmen teach in the churches, but it is good northern talk, all the same. No true man can live without vengeance; it is meat and drink. It keeps him going when life is harsh. Now sit and drink more of the good beer before it goes cold.'

With his cup at his lips, Hereward suddenly said, 'I remember now—they were Englishmen. But their names will not come to my tongue.'

The other said, 'Drink, drink, drink, man! Their names will come to you when you meet them again. And then I hope I am beside you, for three against one is too much in the scales. But we two together—that will be a fight for them to tell their grand-children of.'

Hereward wiped his lips of the beer and said, 'After I have met them, they will tell no one of the meeting.'

The big man laughed, and soon afterwards they rolled up in blankets on the straw and went to sleep.

Late on the next day they came down to a deserted inlet where no steadings were, and only the hungry gulls made a sound, wheeling and crying in their harsh, timeless voices over the rocks and the salt breakers.

Tucked away in the little haven was a longship, and men aboard wrapped in bear-skins and crouched over braziers, as though they had been waiting for some days.

When they saw the big man they stood up and waved their hands or their swords at him.

One of them, a black-bearded elderly man with only one eye, shouted, 'You have been long enough, Hardrada. We thought Swein had you in his dungeons and we were coming to look for you. Come on and let's be away. The tide is right.'

Hereward stopped and looked at his companion. Then he went on to his knees before him, memory flooding back to him.

'Hardrada,' he said, '*that* is who you are! God save me, I should have known. There is only one like you in the world.'

Harald Hardrada put his hands under Hereward's armpits and lifted him as easily as he would a child.

'Never kneel before me, Griffog,' he said. 'I am only half a king yet. My nephew, Magnus, still holds the throne of Norway. But it will be mine one day. I am his heir. In the meantime, I am a soldier who likes to have fearless men about him. Come now and shake hands with my shipmaster, Karr. He shall fit you out with sword and helm and byrnie. Then we shall sail, Odin and the Whitechrist willing, to Tunsberg. Who knows, King Magnus might be ready to let me have my share of the kingdom now!'

So Hereward and Harald Hardrada sailed to Norway that winter, although few others would have dared the Skager Rak at such a time of the year.

It was over six years since Hereward had met Kormac at Holmganga, and the time had passed like one day; a dark day, with a sunny afternoon.

Part Two

1047 - 1068

7. Hardrada's
Judgement and the Melon

THAT YEAR King Magnus died suddenly while foraging in
Denmark and was soon forgotten by most of the fierce men of
Norway. So Harald Hardrada, though he spoke few gentle words
to any but his own lords and carles, became the Hero of the North
and King of Norway, in his nephew's place.

Sometimes, at his Folk Moots held in the various towns and
even villages, men would come to him with their problems and
grievances as his favoured carles squatted about his chair. Once a
black-browed franklin stood before him and said, 'King, three of
my thralls have run away, over the hill to the steading of my
neighbour, Herlief of Stavanger. They will not return, nor will
he give them back. I ask judgement.'

King Harald said, 'Are they men or women, man?'

The franklin said, 'A pretty girl and her two strong brothers,
King.'

'No doubt the pretty girl will marry well; and no doubt the

two strong brothers would fight any man who tried to take them back?'

The franklin nodded.

Harald said, 'Then, as good Christians, let us be both charitable and wise to our health, friend. Let the girl marry the hero she will find and live happily with him; and do not let us bait the brothers lest they take up an axe and split our heads. Leave them be.'

The franklin began to bite his knuckles and say, 'But what do I receive for them? Herlief is not a rich man, lord.'

'That being so, let him pay one hen and two brave cocks. The one for the girl, the others for the brothers.'

When the franklin began to wave his big head about and clench his red fists in anger, the King said, 'You asked for my counsel, and you have got it. It may seem hard counsel, but it has been spoken now in the presence of witnesses. We are now on to another page of the book; the story of the franklin who threatened a king. Once this happened in the days of the good Saint Olaf; so Olaf, my kinsman, sent this man to pray on his knees for forty days and nights, with only bread and water, in Jerusalem. And the prayer was that one day kings should deliver better justice. If you think I have been unjust, then I command you to sell all you have, to put your wife and daughters in the care of the Church, and to pray for me in Jerusalem for forty days and nights without ceasing. I will send a carle with you to see that you do not fall asleep and so bring dishonour to yourself in the Holy Church there. What say you, franklin?'

The man fell on to his knees and said, 'I accept your counsel, Harald. Let the three stay with Herlief.'

Another time a monk came rushing into the King's steading at the time of judgement and said, 'Harald, a young boy whom I have been teaching to read and write for three years has joined a shipload of Vikings to sail to Greenland. The Church paid his father good money for this boy, to make him a priest. I have spent many hours teaching him to read and write. He should be brought back. Send for him before the longship sails, lord.'

Harald Hardrada said, 'Look at you, brother; you are fifty at least, and have forgotten what a young boy likes. Your arms are thin and your eyes are weak. You have never known the joy of axe-play, or the thrill of searching the far salt-horizon for new lands. As for this reading and writing you speak of, what are they, set beside horses and byrnies? Just air, and bad air at that! My purse-keeper shall pay the Church what the Church once paid the boy's father. So he will be free; then one day he may come back to you with a present of carved walrus ivory. Or even a book in some foreign tongue, full of writing, that will give your brain something new to bite on. Our young men are always going into foreign churches and bringing back such things.'

The monk said, 'I want nothing that is stolen, lord.'

'Brother, you and I steal the air we breathe. It belongs by right to God.'

'But think of the time I have wasted with this boy.'

'Men are always wasting time. It is a human condition, friend. I wasted time waiting for this kingdom while Magnus sat on the throne. Edward of England wastes time building a great Minster in London—he has enough churches already. My carles waste time telling tales of ancient warriors. And you waste time coming to me this morning, when I have a year's taxes to count out. I bid you go away and pray for me; I am a stupid man and need your prayers. The boy who ran away will not need them for another forty years.'

This sort of hard counsel was given by the King at every court he held. Yet the people loved him for it—all except the grasping jarls and the greedy priests.

One night, in a barn near the sea, Harald said to Hereward, 'Well, you have heard my judgements these five years. What do you think of me?'

He often teased Hereward in this friendly way, before the other carles, because the answers were sometimes amusing.

This time Hereward said, 'I own nothing but the hole in my head. Even my sword and byrnie are the king's. So I can speak without fear or favour, Harald. You can have the hole in my head, if you want it.'

King Harald said, 'You mean to say that I take everything from everyone, hey, Griffog?'

Hereward said, 'Not exactly, Harald. I saw an old woman swallow a hen's egg yesterday. And she seemed to relish it, what is more. You did not take that from her; and if you want to take it now, you are too late, I would guess.'

All the carles laughed at this, and filled Hereward's drinking-horn again. Even the King laughed and said, 'I am well answered, Griffog. So you think I hold Norway in my hand and squeeze it dry?'

Hereward said, 'You hold it in your hand, certainly. But maybe Swein of Denmark would squeeze it drier, lord. Better the hand which only holds hard than the one which pinches.'

King Harald nodded, pleased that his friend was so forthright and honest. He said, 'Do you regret serving me, Welshman?'

And Hereward answered, 'Does a man regret the wind that blows his ship along, or the sun that ripens his harvest? Ask me no more, Harald. I cannot talk and drink at the same time.'

Then he turned his back on the King and began to play with a dog that lay on the hearth. She was a bitch named Elsa and had a fine litter of puppies. All puppies and kittens and children would let Hereward handle them; and they all seemed to understand the gentle words he spoke to them. Once an old carle named Storkud bent over Hereward while he was talking to a newly-born calf and said, 'What language is that you speak? I cannot understand it.'

Hereward said, 'The calf cannot understand the language I speak to you—so all is fair.'

No one could get the better of Hereward in these crack-brained arguments. It was as though a different sort of sense had come into his head through that hole.

On the other hand, a new sort of nonsense had come, too. If the summer was too hot, or the winter too icy, this seemed to affect him, and then men had to be wary. He would flare into a mighty rage over the smallest thing—like someone telling him that his shoe was unlaced, or that a speck of rust was growing on the shoulder of his byrnie. He once half-throttled a famous carle who had only pointed out that the leg of the stool that Hereward sat on was cracked.

Usually men knew when these moods were coming over him, because at such times he would spend hours burnishing his new sword that Harald had given him. And always he hissed like a serpent while he did this.

Then men left him alone. All except Hardrada, who would sit beside him and burnish his own sword, Brynthvari, the Mail-piercer. Hereward never quarrelled with the King, but often told him that Brynthvari wasn't sharp enough to cut through a piece of butter. One evening Harald said, 'That may be so, old one, but I can tell you that it will cut through a melon.'

Hereward stopped burnishing and said, 'A melon? What is that nonsense, Harald? What is a melon? I have never seen one. Why has no one ever shown me a melon?'

Harald said, 'Because there are none in the north. A melon is as big as a man's head; it is a fruit whose flesh is so tender that it melts in the mouth. Its juice runs down a man's beard. That is a melon.'

Three nights later Hereward came to the King and said, 'I have dreamed only of melons since you last spoke, Harald. Tell me, do they have faces, with a nose and eyes? That is how I see them in my dreams.'

Harald shook his head and said, 'I have eaten melons in Ascalon and Tyre, but have never seen one with a face, friend.'

Hereward went away, but returned later when the King was planning to build a church, with all the bishops round him. He said, 'Harald, put that scroll to one side for a while, I want to ask you something. If a melon has no face, how does one melon know another?'

The bishops began to laugh at this, but Harald silenced them with a grim look and nodded to them to leave the chamber.

When they were alone Harald said to Hereward, 'Look, friend, this is no way to go on. These good bishops have travelled many miles through the snow to plan their church with me. One of them who started out was even eaten by the wolves. You are not being fair to them, to break in with this talk of melons.'

Hereward sat on a little stool at the King's feet and said, 'I am sorry, Harald, but there are some things a man has to know, or he will go mad. Each night, in my dreams, I see the faceless melons trying to find their husbands or wives. It will send me mad, King. Show me but one melon, and I will vow to kill all the wolves between here and Bergen. Then the ghost of the dead old bishop will be pacified.'

King Harald scratched his beard, then said, 'Griffog, my dear stupid one, melons are not alive as men are, so they have no wives; they have no feet, so they cannot go searching. As for the old bishop, he was too holy a man to have a gibbering ghost. As for the wolves, they might kill you, and not you them; and that would be a bad bargain for me, because you are now my most trusted carle.'

Hereward began to nod his head backwards and forwards. So Harald said, 'Look man, forget about melons. I am sorry I ever mentioned them. Forget them and I will make you captain of my carles. How is that?'

Hereward said, 'Lord, that would please me well—but I would still like to see a melon. I shall not rest until I do.'

It was a week later, when the ice was melting in the rivers, that Harald sent for Hereward and said, 'Very well, captain, you *shall* see a melon. News has come to me that my wife in Kiev is sick, so we will sail down the great rivers and visit her. From Kiev it is but a short way to Miklagard. There in the markets are armies of melons. How would that please you, friend?'

Hereward kneeled and kissed the King's hand. This was unusual for him—he did not often feel so moved.

King Harald left Norway in the charge of his son, Olaf, and when the ships were tarred and their sails patched set off to the south. It was summer before they reached Kiev, and found that Harald's wife, Elizabeth, was dead. The King of Norway had prayers said for a hundred days in her memory, then travelled on towards Miklagard.

Hereward was not sorry to leave Kiev. The streets were too narrow to breathe in, he said; and the houses were so high that they seemed about to fall on one. Besides, rats came up from the river into the carles' lodgings and ate their horse-hide tunics in the night. Next, they would eat the sword-scabbards, Hereward told the King; and then the swords would rust. And then the carles would be weaponless. And then the men with tall sheepskin hats, who always rode along the river banks watching the longships, would be able to kill them all.

Hereward did not like these men, largely because they covered their bodies with mutton-fat and their eyes were black beads glittering through slits in their yellow skin. He thought they must all be wizards. Harald, who knew these men well and could even speak their language after a fashion, told Hereward that they were a wandering folk called Patzinaks, and were harmless as long as men left them alone. They only fought if attacked—and then they were furious fighters with little horn bows that could shoot arrows a great distance. Hereward said, 'Why do they follow us, then?'

The King answered, 'They are an inquisitive folk. They think we are ghosts, with our pale hair and white skins. They have no longships like us and want to find out how ghosts float upon the water.'

Hereward said, 'They must be crack-brained then.'

This made a number of the carles laugh, but Hereward did not know why.

They reached Miklagard in late summer, after the sun had lost most of its fierce heat. This suited the Vikings well.

8. Miklagard

MOST OF Harald's men had never seen Miklagard before. To them, the great harbour with its white stones and many-coloured sails seemed wonderful. Others admired the high city walls with their round look-out towers. But all were struck with amazement once the great gates were opened to them; for they saw bright-flowered gardens, more church spires than they could count, camels laden with merchandise shuffling down the long straight avenues, and the marble cupolas of the Imperial palace which seemed to touch the blue sky itself.

A troop of dark-skinned horsemen cantered across the Square of St Sophia, laughing and showing their white teeth. Their captain was not swarthy, but as red-faced as any of the northmen. He wore his yellow plaits almost down to his waist, though the helmet on his head was made after the ancient Greek manner, with a high plume of trimmed horsehair. He swept his eyes over the clustering northmen, then called to his troop to halt. He trotted his great black horse over to where they stood and swung out of the gilded saddle.

'Why, Harald,' he said. 'What brings you to Miklagard? Have you come to sign on again with the Guard? I'll promise you, the Emperor would weep with joy to have such a band of Varangers again! It is many years since you left us, and we have never had such a captain since. All we get these days are cattle like those who sit behind me—Arabs who call themselves Christians, but change sides the moment the first arrows fly; or Armenians who turn and run if they see a sword come out of the sheath. This is good, this meeting.'

But, when they had done embracing each other, Harald said, 'Nay, Thord, I have done with fighting for other men. Now I look only after myself. We are in Miklagard to look round a little and to see the beauty of the world. I have a carle here, a Welshman called Griffog, who has never seen a melon. So we come to see these fruits and to let their juice run down our beards.'

Thord slapped his thigh and began to laugh. 'Always the same Harald,' he said. 'Once you came to see the horse-fights in the Hippodrome, remember? And you stayed for ten years! The old Emperor Constantine Monomachus never forgave you for trying to run off with young Anastasia! As for old Zoë, she even got the Patriarch to invent torments for you, if ever your ships were caught! But it passed over, as all things do in Byzantium, and now you would be as welcome as the first aconite of spring.'

But Harald shook his great head and said, 'The smell of incense sickens me, Thord. The water of my own mountain streams tastes better than your wine. The pay here was never too good, and up north a man can always find himself a coffer of gold and a few acres of land, if he likes to look round a bit. Besides, I have a wife or two, here and there, and I like to be able to visit them from time to time.'

That evening, when the carles sat drinking and singing in a tavern near the Avenue of Justinian, the door opened and a young woman came in. She was dressed in a robe of fine white samite, over which was a hood and cloak of blue gauze. This did not hide her shining blue-black hair, nor the oval ivory-white face with its big dark eyes. In a semicircle hanging on her forehead were gold

coins on a silver chain. They jingled as she bent to greet Harald.
'I am Euphemia, lord,' she said. 'My grandfather was your old battle-friend, Wolf Glismakson, who came from Iceland. My father was an emir among the Seljuks. Now they are dead and Thord, the captain, has sent me to be your wife.'

Harald raised the girl and pulled a stool out with his foot for her to sit on. He said, 'My dear, there was a time when you could have kept me in Miklagard with your loveliness; but I am a busy king in the north now, and have many things to see to. Drink a little wine with us, and then go back to Thord and tell him there is no one I would sooner marry—but other things have been decreed for me by God, and I must go.'

Euphemia began to look downcast, so Harald said, 'Look, girl, it is not because I do not admire you. You are beautiful; I say that, who have looked at hundreds of princesses in my day. It is just that . . .'

The girl began to rock backwards and forwards and to clutch Harald by the knees. 'If you do not take me,' she said, 'my uncle will place me in a convent, and I shall never dance or sing in the sun again.'

Harald was looking so worried that Hereward went up and placed his hand on the girl's shoulder. 'Harald,' he said, 'I came down to Miklagard to see the melons, but instead I see the most lovely woman a man has ever clapped eyes on. Let me take this lady as my wife, and I will put melons out of my thoughts. Is that a bargain?'

Harald looked relieved, but said, 'The lady has to agree first, Griffog. I do not intend to run away from Miklagard this time, with the harbour chains drawn across to keep me in!'

Hereward looked into the girl's eyes and said, 'I look old—but each year I am getting younger. I sound a fool—but each day I am getting wiser. I would love and honour you; will you have me?'

Euphemia suddenly began to cry out loud, then knelt and touched Hereward's feet with her smooth ivory forehead.

'I will take you as my lord,' she said. 'And gladly.'

So Hereward got himself a wife. They were married the next

day in a side-chapel of St Sophia by a priest who had once served in Kiev and knew the sort of ceremony that northmen liked.

There was no dowry from Euphemia, and no wedding-gift from Hereward. They became man and wife in the clothes they stood up in—except that Hereward had to leave his sword outside the chapel while the holy water was poured over him. King Harald of Norway paid the marriage-fee to the Church. It was fifty bezants, which he got by selling the wolf-skin jacket off his back in the market. It was the fashion at that time to have something from the mysterious north hanging on one's walls. A young Greek courtier-lord bought the wolf-skin and was glad to get it at the price.

Hereward was glad, too, because he had come to the age of forty and had never before seen the woman he would want to marry. Euphemia was as pretty as a bird and as merry as a cricket; just the woman to make a man feel like a boy again. The rough carles adored her; and when she was not mending their jerkins and breeches with her nimble needle, she was playing to them on her little lute; or teaching them a game called 'cat in the corner'. It was a simple game, right for simple soldiers—not wearing to the brain, like chess. They played it in all the rooms of the tavern until the Syrian innkeeper complained that they were driving his customers away, lurking in dark corners and then jumping out and yelling in their loud northern voices, 'You're *it*! You're the cat! Off with your tail!'

Some guests from Egypt, who still held the cat as a sacred beast, did not like this. But much good did their complaining do them among the northmen! Euphemia giggled out of her upper window to see these protesting ambassadors climbing, wet through, out of the fountain in the little courtyard.

At last Harald said, 'It is time for us to set the prows to the north, my carles. Soon the Dnieper will be frozen and the portages will be windswept. Let us be off.'

And so they went, early one Thursday morning. Thor had blessed the day, for the sun shone across the Bosporus as though only gold and good fortune lay before them.

At Kiev, Euphemia told Hereward that, God willing, they

59

might have a baby to take home with them to Norway. He was so glad that he sold his dagger and his bear-skin cloak to buy ale for any man who would drink the child's health in the inn on Jaroslav Square. He would have sold his sword, too, in his mad joy; but King Harald became very stern and said that this was one thing a carle never did—not even to buy Masses for the soul of his father.

The going was slow and the baby came when they reached Smolensk. It was a fine boy and they called him Cnut, after the old King of England. It was during the christening that Hereward first revealed to King Harald that his own name was not Griffog, and that he was not a Welshman. This had to be done, because the priest was a precise old man who wanted to know the why's and the wherefore's of everything.

At the christening feast, Harald laughed and said, 'Well, Hereward, you can't be so daft if you can keep a secret as long as that!'

Hereward looked at him clearly and answered, 'Harald, I feel better now than I have ever felt. Memories have come back to me all the time. The darkness has quite gone from me. For me, now, life is a pretty thing—and I think that if I were set face to face with Giant Kormac once more, at the holmgang, I would not wish to hurt him—and certainly not for that old shrew, Gunhilda! Indeed, I love all men.'

9. Bad News

THEN ILL luck struck the voyagers. Winter came without warning and the northmen, overhasty in rolling their longships across the portage from Smolensk to the River Dvina, stove two of them in. Though there were forests nearby, the shipwrights could not work in blinding snowstorms. The only thing to do was to up-end the other ships and use them as huts until spring came. So they fought off wolves and wandering outlaws from Novgorod way, and fed on reindeer and even bear-meat.

Little Cnut was walking by himself before they sailed down the Dvina; and he was talking a language men could understand when they reached Kurland.

But here they were delayed again. Both Euphemia and Hardrada fell sick with pains in the chest and much coughing, brought on, the doctors said, by the bitter winter they had suffered.

During the many months at Kurland, Hereward spent much time with his little son, riding the boy on his back, teaching him how to fish, and even trying to show him how to fight with a small whalebone sword that one of the men had fashioned for him. Euphemia put a stop to this when she was well again. 'Husband,' she said, 'I will not have the boy spoiled. You will make him grow up wild and headstrong. He is only three, and already he disobeys me.'

Hardrada heard this and laughed. 'Why, lady,' he said, 'have you never heard that my kinsman, Olaf the Holy, drank mead at six weeks, rode a horse before he could walk, and killed a bear on his second birthday?'

He and Hereward were slapping each other on the back at these silly words when a man came in, footsore with journeying, his ears bitten by the frost, his right arm in a bloody sling.

He said, 'King Harald, you have been away too long. Swein of Denmark has burned too many of our steadings. And there is worse than that.'

Harald sat the man in a chair and gave him warm mead to drink, for his chin was shivering so badly that his words were not clear.

'Tell me,' he said.

After a while the man said, 'While you have been away, the world has turned upside down. No more and no less. No one knows who is king and who is thrall, wherever you like to look, in whatever land. Some rebels say that Swein should be King in Norway; some say that Duke William the Norman should be King in England; some say that Harold Godwinson should be the Hero of the North, that you have foregone that title.'

There was a fine cup of silver and crystal on the table. King Harald took it in his hand and squeezed it until it shattered and the precious stones flew out of their metal casing. Then he flung it into the hearth and gritted his teeth.

Hereward took up an ash stave as thick as a man's wrist that was used to beat cows out of the feast-hall, and broke it with one twist of his hands. He and Harald made such a noise of grinding their teeth that it was painful to hear.

Harald said, 'There is only one Hero of the North, and he sits in this room now.'

Hereward said, 'When I promised to love all men, I did not mean the kin of Godwine. They are not men, but wolves.'

The messenger put down his mead-cup and said, 'That may be so; but there is one of the brood waiting for you in Norway. He swears that if you will help him kill his brother, he will see to it that Harald Hardrada is never troubled again.'

King Harald just stared at the man with eyes like pieces of grey glass. The man said, 'Tostig Godwinson, once Earl of Northumbria, has come to you, Harald, and asks you to help him regain his earldom and even the crown of England.'

Harald said, 'Has England not got a King? Does not old Edward still mumble his prayers in his new Minster?'

The messenger shook his head and said, 'Old Edward has died. He was buried in his Minster on Twelfth Day, with the snow on his coffin. Now Harold Godwinson is King in England and has had his coinage struck in forty places. The excommunicated Bishop Stigand has consecrated him; the Witan have promised to obey him in all things. And he has vowed to put an end to Tostig, and to you!'

King Harald Hardrada said at last, 'I do not love Tostig—but I love his brother Harold still less. There is only one way to deal with a wolf—and that is to kill it and nail its hide on the barn door. This we shall do.'

The messenger said, 'The world is full of trouble, Harald. There are other wolves besides Harold Godwinson. The Pope has given his blessing to Duke William the Norman, and has sent him banners and the Cross of the Apostle in silver and gold, as a sign that he is the rightful King of England. So, you will still have William to deal with when you have killed Wolf Harold.'

Hardrada said, 'Better the Norman than the son of Godwine. I have spoken with William before and know that, at least, he is a man—and not a sneaking hedge-thief. We will put an end to the Godwine, and then, mayhap, if the dice fall right, I will divide England between Tostig and Duke William, with myself as overlord.'

Hereward said quietly, 'Better destroy them all, and put on the throne the lad who has most right to be king—Edgar the Atheling, the grandson of old Edmund Ironside—and the true heir to the throne. He is said to be a comely youth, and with good advisers might bring peace to England.'

But Hardrada was not listening. He was already planning to cross the sea back to Norway and begin his preparations.

10. Earl Tostig

THE CROSSING to Norway was a rough one. On that voyage many of the carles who called themselves Christians openly fell to their knees and asked the aid of Odin; and King Harald did nothing to stop them.

Euphemia was with little Cnut in the after-part of the longship, where the king had placed a striped awning to give her privacy. She looked up with her great dark eyes and said to Hereward, 'Husband, God has been good to us, bringing us together and giving us a son. Now there is talk of war, and I know well enough that in war men are killed and do not return to their homes. I count myself lucky to have found you, by God's help; would it not be wickedness to place yourself in such danger that Cnut and I might lose you?'

Hereward bit his lip and answered, 'Euphemia, lovely one, I am a sworn carle and must serve my master, the King. Harald made me into a man again when I was only a thrall in a steading where the rain dripped through the rotten thatch. He gave me rings and byrnie, sword and shield. In a way, guided by God no doubt, he even gave me you. So there is a debt I must pay him. If Harald wishes to become great in the north and to hold part of England, it is my duty to follow him.'

Euphemia bowed her head, obedient after the manner of the women who had known Eastern teaching. All the same, she whispered, 'Have you no duty to your son and your wife who adores you, Hereward? Would it not be wiser to leave the service of the king and set up as a peaceful farmer in Norway? You are rich enough now, surely. And we could live simply and do no harm to anyone. You could put your sword away and forget that your hand had ever guided it.'

Hereward was so troubled by her words that he strode about the little space and punched his hands together. At last he said, 'There is something else, Euphemia. Years ago the Godwines hurt me by treachery. They took away from me my senses for a while, made me an old man before my time. In the deeps of my heart, I do not care if King Harald of Norway holds this kingdom or that—but I do care that the Godwine brood should know I have come for my payment, my revenge.'

Cnut was frightened by his father's shouting and began to cry, so Hereward held him, bobbing him up and down and singing songs to him.

Euphemia said, 'Husband, you talk like a savage. Revenge is empty; it eats a man's heart away and leaves him a husk. Let us forget revenge; let us go anywhere to be away from it, I beg you.'

Hereward said slowly, 'My love, my only love, you are asking me to forget my nature. Can you ask a seal to grow wings and fly through the air; or a snake to put on legs and walk? You are asking me to say that it is not dark at night, or light by day. You cannot turn the sun into the moon by asking, my dear.'

Euphemia began to cry then, and Cnut joined with her. Hereward felt the old wound beginning to throb in his head. He put the boy down beside Euphemia on the bed and said, 'Wherever a carle goes in this world he will find wars to be fought, if he is a man. In Denmark the young boys have prepared for war since they can remember. In Flanders a man would be torn many ways—whether to fight for this one or that. In Normandy the proud duke dreams of conquering the world. In Ireland northmen squabble with all others. Even distant Iceland is full of outlaws and robber-men, who will knife each other for the price of a sheep. The world is like a boiling-pot, Euphemia. And it will not stop bubbling until the fire beneath it is quenched. Now if Hardrada can gain power in England and destroy the Godwines, some of the fire might well be doused. Let us say that Hardrada might share England with Duke William; why, then there would be peace in that land, and we might find ourselves a place to live quietly. Or say that we do not choose to live there—well, once I have helped the king and helped to destroy my enemies, then you and I, with the bounty I shall gain, could sail down the big rivers again and live in Kiev or even in Miklagard. There would be room for us there.'

Euphemia saw that it was no good arguing with her husband. So she gathered her son to her and curled up. Hereward thought they were asleep, so kissed them both and went forward to where Hardrada stood at the bucking prow.

Hardrada said, 'So that is settled. I could hear your words

through the awning, above the splash of the salt sea. A linen awning is not like a wooden wall, carle.'

Hereward felt a little ashamed, but could not say anything. Hardrada said, 'Women get in the way, even the most lovely of them. It has been my habit to marry them, then leave them behind in some place where they could not disturb my thoughts. It is good to visit them from time to time, to get news of one's sons; but not to carry such bickerings with one into battle. A fighting man needs all his thought for the enemy. Perhaps I did wrong in taking you down to Miklagard to taste a melon. It would have paid me to send a trader on the journey for a load of the things; then your mind would not have been divided.'

He smiled, the spray lashing his red face, turning it redder. A white gull swept low over the ship and squawked out as though it was laughing at these men who rocked on the grey seas in a wooden shell and thought they could rule the world.

Hereward said at last, 'Harald, a man can only go to meet his fate; whether it is murder or melons, swords or sweetmeats. I go now with you to meet my fate, to meet Tostig. But after the meeting is over, after this battle is done, I shall give my heart and mind to my wife and my son. I shall ask you to release me from my oath and to let me be my own man again, to build my own house and arrange my own life. Is that agreed?'

Harald Hardrada nodded, his mouth tightened into a grim smile. 'It is agreed,' he said. 'This is what I have known all my life. Men have knelt before me, have traded blows alongside me—and then they have left me. Only I have gone on, and on, half-way across the world. I have a dream. My dream is to rule the north— I alone, with no popes or priests or counsellors to tell me how it should be done. This is my great chance. If I aid Tostig now, all could be mine—from Iceland to Brittany. *All of it!* No northman has ever held such dice in his hand—and all for one throw.'

He glanced at Hereward then and said with a strange smile, 'And all who come with me on this journey to power will be remembered. And all who stand against me will be known. They will not escape, though they set sail for Greenland or Egypt. There

66

will be no corner in the earth small enough to hide them.'

The gull wheeled about the ship once more, laughing. And Hardrada said, 'For you, Hereward, there will be a prince's domain. Think of that. Once this affair is done, you can place your sword-point on any part of the map, from Orkney to Novgorod, and I will see that there is a throne for you to sit on, and lands for you to rule. Is that enough?'

Hereward bowed his head and said, 'It is enough, lord. I will come with you this once—and may Odin give us victory.'

Then he went back to the awning, because little Cnut was crying once more.

They landed quietly in Uppsala the next day, and went as traders across the hills, their swords and byrnies wrapped in cow-hides. They came to Hardrada's hall a week later.

Here Hereward first met Tostig Godwinson. He was a great barrel-chested man, with a black beard that crept up his cheeks to his eyelids. He was very merry and laughed whenever he spoke. No man would have taken him for a son of old Earl Godwine. He even spoke with a Norman accent and not an English one, and all the men took to him straightway.

When Hereward stood before him, Tostig said, 'You are the man my kinsfolk quarrelled with. I have heard the tale up and down the land. Well, you are still alive—which is more than might be expected. It is not often that my brothers make that sort of mistake. Now you can stand before brother Harold once more and tell him what you think of him.'

Hereward stared Tostig in the eye and said, 'When I stand before him, I shall not speak to him. Only this sword will speak, and Harold Godwinson will not care to hear the words it will say.'

Tostig pulled at his beard and said quietly, 'I admire a man with a purpose in life; but let me warn you, do not stand too close to brother Harold to deliver your message. He, too, has been known to make the sword-edge deliver a message of some wit.'

Then he began to laugh again and to pat Cnut on the cheek and to admire the beauty of Euphemia for all to hear. Euphemia blushed with pleasure, and Hardrada stood behind her, his bear-like paw upon her shoulder. Hereward felt proud that such great ones should treat his wife and son with honour.

That night, in their room, he said to her, 'I have heard all manner of evil spoken about Tostig Godwinson; but it seems to me that he is a man I could follow.'

Euphemia said, 'In Miklagard, such a man would stand beside the Emperor himself. Husband, it seems to me that he and Hardrada are truly great men, the greatest in the north.'

Hereward pretended to be annoyed and said, 'And what of your own husband, Saracen woman?'

Euphemia said with a smile, 'Very well, then you should stand behind the Emperor. And perhaps Duke William of Normandy might have a place beside *you*. Then there would be five great men in the world. Will that do?'

Hereward nodded. 'That will do,' he said. 'As long as you do not add Harold Godwinson to the company. There is not room for us and him in the world.'

Before dawn the next day they were wakened by the galloping of horses. A thrall came in and said, 'Tostig has gone, master. He and our king have made their vows to each other, and will meet with all their forces, either in Scotland, or by the Tyne, or by the Humber. They will take York first, and then bring back the old Northern rule in England. One day, mayhap, we shall all feast in London.'

Hereward said, 'You hear too much for a thrall. Be off with you, man, and say these words to no one else.'

The thrall said, 'I only speak to kings and captains, lord.'

Hereward laughed, but Euphemia's face was troubled.

'What will happen to us, husband, while you are away?' she said.

Hereward smothered her puzzled brow with kisses. 'Dearest,' he replied, 'you and the little warrior, Cnut, will sit here snug by the fire until I send for you. Then, in York or Lincoln or London—it matters not where—we shall have a great rejoicing. You shall wear a robe of silk and a little gold crown upon your head. My son, my blessed little mouse here, shall have Harold Godwinson's dagger to play with!'

Euphemia began to laugh. 'You are still a fool,' she said. 'What would Cnut want with a dagger!'

11. Stamfordbridge

IT WAS a bright sunny day; and though it was September it might have been high summer, for the sun beat down so much upon the meadows that the northmen took off their helmets and byrnies, even their wool vests and trousers and, leaving their swords and shields in a pile, stretched out like boys and let their tired bodies drink it in, as a cloth drinks water.

Half of their army rested on the other side of the lazy, narrow River Derwent, listening to the water lapping and the late birds singing, giving praise to God that they had so easily landed on English soil and had been allowed the good fortune to capture the city of York.

Hereward sat with Harald Hardrada, and near them lay men of many sorts; northmen from Ireland, berserks of Sognefiord where they had all sailed from, Flemings sent by Baldwin of Flanders—anxious to be on the winning side—and even Scots who had come down at the command of their King, Malcolm Bighead, who was said to know all things—even the language of frogs.

'He needs to,' had whispered one old carle from Bergen. 'Most of his subjects are frogs. Frogs and heath-adders!'

On the far side of the river lay Tostig and some of Harald's foragers, including many men from Shetland and Orkney. They had come with seventeen ships and three good battle-leaders—Copsi who had once been Earl of Northumbria, and the Earls Paul and Erling. These men of the far north had given a good account of themselves near York, at Fulford, against the English forces. Earl Erling carried more wounds than a hedgehog had quills, men said, and none of them serious, by the grace of God! Nothing that would not have healed by the time he sailed back to the north and put his arms about his new young wife who waited for him there, in the windblown dust.

What amused Erling most was that Earl Paul, who had been biting the shield-rim and foaming at the lips all the way down to Yorkshire, boasting how many heads he would take and how much trophy from the churches in York, had been left behind at Riccall on the Ouse, to guard Hardrada's three hundred ships; but really to guard Hardrada's son, the Prince Olaf, who was with him there. A wise woman had foretold that Prince Olaf should not meet the English leaders, the Earls Edwin and Morcar, in battle. So Hardrada had commanded his son to stay ten miles away by road from York.

In the meadow by the river Hereward leaned on his elbow and nibbled at a blade of grass. Hardrada said, smiling, 'What is it, captain? You were shouting loud enough in the arrow-hail yesterday, and singing like a lark among the spears the day before. And, don't you recall, as we rode into York you vowed to take Morcar's palace from him and set up there with your dear wife, Euphemia, and your son?'

Hereward smiled and said, 'It is of them I am thinking. I hope Euphemia keeps warm while we are away. The sea-fret that sweeps into Bergen is bad for the chest, and she, being from the south, takes cold easily, as you know.'

Hardrada said, 'No thought for little Cnut, then?'

Hereward threw the grass-stalk away and said, 'I think of him

70

every moment. Even when the arrows comb my hair and the swords tickle my throat. I hope that Euphemia can find cow's milk for him in Bergen; that goat's milk turns the lad's stomach.'

A Scot, whose face was painted with streaks of blue dye, said to another, 'Hear that? These terrible Vikings talk about goat's milk when they should be shouting of blood and plunder! Our churchmen have told us wrong about them!'

Both Hereward and Hardrada turned to gaze at the man. After a moment, he could stand their cold eyes no longer and moved away.

Hereward said, 'It is just as well. In another minute his head would have floated down the river.'

Hardrada nodded. 'I should have done it if you had not, friend. I wonder if we were wise to bring these Scots with us,' he said quietly. 'They quickly forget the plan of attack, and think only of what they can seize before they run away again. That is no way to conduct a war, especially when the throne of England is our goal.'

Hereward thought for a while, then said, 'All goes well. When the Earls Edwin and Morcar have surrendered hostages to us and a fair share of treasure from York, then we can turn south and take London. King Harold Godwinson, curse his name, must be shivering in his shoes now, holding his sister's hand in the new Minster there, and wondering which of us will strike first— Hardrada or Duke William of Normandy!'

But Hardrada had stopped listening. He was saying, 'That is a strange omen, friend. A country with three queens in it. Or as good as queens! There is Godwinson's mother, Gytha; there is his first wife, Edith Swansneck; and there is Ealdgytha, his second wife, sister of Earl Edwin. In Norway this would make a king afraid—three queens living. We say that there are only three queens allowed by Odin when a king has to be carried away in a death-barge, like the old British king, Arthur.'

Hereward nodded and chose another stalk of grass to chew. 'I do not think Godwinson need fear that,' he said. 'His wife, Edith Swansneck, was never married to him in church. They just shook hands before their friends and said they would be man and wife. She is not even called queen. Nor is his mother, Gytha. She only acts like a queen!'

Hardrada, who never liked to be bested in an argument, said, 'Very well, then, there is one who cannot be denied—and I had forgotten her. There is Harold's own sister, the widow of Edward the Confessor. *That* makes three queens. Now do you agree?'

Hereward grinned and said, 'You best me, Harald. So perhaps there are three queens in England. Let us hope that they are getting the black barge painted and ready on the Thames at this moment. I am tired of voyaging and exchanging sword-blows. The sooner they row Godwinson away with muffled oars, the better for me. Then I can settle down and see what it is like to grow barley and milk my own cows.'

But Hardrada was gazing away from him, not listening, his eyes fixed on a grassy ridge less than a quarter of a mile away. Hereward followed his lord's stare and saw men coming over the ridge. They were carrying spears, and the sun glinted on their helmets and mesh-shirts. In their midst fluttered two banners—one bearing the figure of the great dragon of Wessex, the other embroidered with a warrior holding a two-handed sword.

Hardrada let out a great cry. 'By Odin,' he said, 'we are betrayed! This is not Edwin and Morcar, come to surrender our spoils. This is Godwinson himself. I have heard of that new banner of his; his mother stitched it with her own hands. It is called the Fighting Man. How can the man have come up from London in so short a time? The devil must be in his heels!'

Now all the men were dragging on their byrnies and helmets, trying to sort out their swords from the pile on the river bank.

The men on the ridge were coming on fast now, shouting like madmen. Hardrada, who could not get his neckplate fastened, turned with a curse and flung it into the river. It fell with a splash so quiet that it was hardly heard. He swung round to Hereward and said, 'This is poor play. There is only one way over this stream, and the water is too deep for a man to walk across. They will trap us by the bridge, where there is no space to swing a dagger, much less a sword.'

A grey-bearded carle from Norway came up to the King then and said, 'You know me, I am Ljot, and this is my axe, Bear's Kiss. I once struck off the heads of three wolves at one blow below Thorkelshill.'

Hardrada was strapping his tall helmet on and said, 'I know you, Ljot. What do you want at this moment, man?'

The northman said, smiling, 'Only the honour of keeping the bridge until you have got your men across to join Tostig. It is a narrow bridge and my axe would keep it clear all day. I merely ask that when the time comes for me to run over after you, the archers will send a hail of arrows to keep Godwinson's dogs from biting me in the back. I have always dreaded ending like that.'

Hardrada said, 'I promise, Ljot. And may Odin ride on your axe-shaft. Kill as many of them as you can; they are of no account in heaven, or Valhalla.'

A strange thing happened then. From the other side of the river, Tostig, hoisted on to the shoulders of two of his thegns, was yelling through cupped hands, 'Harold, brother Harold, this is no way for kinsfolk to act. Call off your men and let there be no bloodshed in these meadows. Before all witnesses, I swear to share England with you, fairly, as set down by honest clerks. Is it a bargain?'

Hardrada said, with a twisted smile, 'Bargain with Godwinson, bargain with a snake! It is the same. If Harold accepts, you and I will not live to see this sun set, friend Hereward.'

Before he had done speaking a hail of arrows fell among them from the men on the ridge. Carles toppled everywhere, clutching at the shafts. A great laugh floated to them from under the Wessex banner.

'It is time to go,' said Hardrada grimly. 'See to it you swing Bear's Kiss wide, friend Ljot. We must have time to form the shield-rings on the other side, and set up my raven banner, Landwaster. Good luck, brother.'

So the northmen and their friends began to run across the bridge, some of them still buckling on their belts.

12. Shield-Ring

IN THE shield-ring, under Landwaster, men jostled together, setting their feet wide, shouting to their comrades to stand away and leave room for axe-swing and sword-play. Carles bundled one another about, like dogs after a bone, for the honour of standing under the banner near to Hardrada. Hereward was closest to the King. They stood smiling together, the sweat running down their faces and on to their shirts. The air was heavy with the sharp smell of damp leather. The wild lavender under their feet flung up its pungent odour as it was crushed to the hot earth. There was another scent in the air, not of leather or lavender, but of men's battle-fury, of that quivering sense of fearfulness that even the bravest of warriors feel just before the blows begin to fall. It was a scent like that of cold steel being ground on the sharpening-stone, no more than that. But once a man caught it in his nostril his teeth chattered and the hair rose upright at the back of his neck.

In the thicket of the shield-ring swords and spears stood like the quills on a hedgehog, almost shutting out the light. King Harald called, 'What of old Ljot? How is he shaking Bear's Kiss now?'

For a while no one answered the King. Then suddenly a man in the foremost shield-rank groaned and shouted back, 'He is down! Ljot is down and into the river. They have got at him from under the planks of the bridge, the dogs!'

Hardrada said in a whisper, 'He has served his turn, poor Ljot! He has held them back long enough. He will dine in Slaughter Hall this evening, among the greatest of the northland.'

Then a carle yelled, 'Stand fast! Wessex is coming now with a vengeance!'

All at once the warm air was filled with a high whining sound, that surged forward as fast as spring rain and then swept on into the distance. Hereward suddenly felt his body streaming wet under his leather shirt and his iron byrnie. It was a cold wet that made him shiver in spite of himself. The King saw this and said, 'You feel it, too, axe-mate? When I was a lad I thought only I felt it, but when I got to talk with old soldiers I learned that they all knew the cold kiss of the Shield Maidens.'

Hereward nodded but did not answer. In his jaws he had clenched the strap of his helmet to keep his teeth from chattering too loudly. He could not speak with the leather in his mouth.

Hardrada saw this also and said, 'The sun stands above us now, friend. But when it sets, behind that dark copse of trees on the ridge, there will be no more sweating, no more biting on the thong. Instead, there will be . . .'

His last words were lost then, because the air was again loud with the arrows' scream and the whole earth seemed to shudder. The outer shield-ring clanged like a great bronze door being beaten with a giant's hammer. A shock like an earthquake struck the men under Landwaster, and hurled them back, one carle against another. Hereward saw the man in front of him falling, his axe swinging, then he also fell back against the King. Hardrada shouted out and propped his shoulders hard against the pole of the banner.

'Hold firm, my lads,' he called, 'or we shall all be on our backs! I did not sail so far to lie stark in an English meadow!'

Hereward heard these words and felt that cold shudder across his back again. He wished the King had not spoken so; it was as though the Norns had used his voice to speak his fate.

Then Hereward had no more time to think of anything but battle, for the carle in front of him fell with his axe under him and then lay still. A tall man, wearing the bronze dragon of Wessex on his helmet, and thrusting with a short boar spear, had broken through the shield-ring and stood less than six feet away. He was squinting, with the sun in his eyes, and showing his great teeth

75

between yellow-bearded lips. 'What I did to the man on the bridge I will do to Hardrada!' he shouted.

Hereward took the spear-thrust in the middle of his linden shield, then swept his sword down in a short swing. The blade glinted in the sunlight like a little rainbow, then jolted as fiercely as an unbroken stallion against Hereward's wrist. He did not need to look at the work it had done. The English carle had gone, down below men's knees, as they stumbled into the darkness. Hereward heard Hardrada laughing behind him, and felt the King pushing at his back and shouting, 'Make way, there! Make way! There will be no battle left for me!'

Hereward found it hard to keep his footing, there were so many men on the ground now and not all of them still and quiet. Once he almost fell down himself, but struggled like a drowning man to keep upright.

Then the tide of battle swung him round and round, away from Landwaster. For a while his eyes were misted with sweat; then, as small and clear as a picture in a silver mirror, he saw Tostig and Harold Godwinson together, swapping blows with axes. They were on a little mound with the sun full on them and their heavy cloaks floating in the wind. Both seemed to be laughing like brothers at play, until suddenly Harold's axe fell where shoulder joins neck, and then Tostig was down, his hands flung wide and defenceless.

A great shout went up, but Hereward could scarcely hear it, his ears were so full of the sound of drumming blood. A big black horse came from nowhere and reared over him, spattering him with foam from its champing jaws. An iron stirrup caught him on the left shoulder, numbing his arm, spinning him about like a boy's top. He caught a glimpse of a red-bearded knight slashing out with an iron mace. Hardly thinking, he parried the blow with his slender sword, and watched the fine blade snap close by the hilt. Then he flung the broken weapon with all his force, and saw the bearded man's mouth open in a soundless cry. Arrows keened in the air again, and all at once it was as though the sky had

darkened before a thunder-clap as the great black horse toppled in
its high prancing and fell down over him.

13. End of an Age

FOR A long while it seemed to Hereward that he was sleeping
through an endless night, broken from time to time by strange
dreams—but dreams so bright, so vivid, that they seemed clearer
and sharper than reality. In these dreams even sounds and scents
came to him; even the waning warmth of the sun upon his
upturned face; and the distant lamentations of curlews to his
ears.

In the first of these dreams he saw the King, Hardrada, lying
on the trampled turf among the crushed wild lavender. The
broken ash pole of Landwaster leaned over him, casting a dark
shadow across the King's body. The linen of the great banner lay
crumpled and ripped and soiled all about, like a sea that waited to
enfold him. Many men stood or knelt round the King, northmen

and Scots and Englishmen; all with pity on their faces, none of them now with swords in their hands.

The King's face was pale and his eyes were dulled. He was breathing harshly, and there was blood down the front of his leather war-shirt. Before this dream faded Hereward saw that the King was holding a little arrow-head in his hand, gazing down on it wearily. And before silence came again Hereward seemed to hear Hardrada say, 'The smith who forged this knew what he was about.' Then the King's hand let fall the arrow-head and his own head slipped down among the billowing folds of Landwaster.

In Hereward's next dream Euphemia and little Cnut were standing over him silently. Euphemia was weeping and letting the tears go, unchecked, down her cheeks. The boy was screwing up his face and whimpering, as though he was hungry. Hereward tried to tell his wife that the lad should be well fed if he was to grow up and become a strong warrior. But she did not seem to hear him; it was as though there were a thick wall of glass between them and no sound reached her ears.

There were other dreams, of Ljot holding the bridge and then flinging away his axe and falling into the river; of the old crone in the steading on the heathland, sitting and crooning to herself by the fire as the wild winds swept over the moors from the sea; there was even a dream of Kormac's face, as he looked down at Hereward on Holmganga. That face wore such a sad expression that Hereward in his dream wished he had never hurt the man with bright Nadr the Serpent.

But although these dreams seemed to last a hundred years, Hereward came out of them at last, into a waking that was so painful that he wished he had slept on.

He was lying across a pony's back, being jolted with every bump of the uneven road. A tall thin man with his right arm in a bandage was walking beside the pony, and when he saw Hereward's eyes open he said hoarsely, 'Courage, man, courage! We shall reach the big river before nightfall, Odin give us grace.'

Hereward said, 'What of the battle, friend? And why am I here?'

The man answered slowly, 'The battle went against us. Hardrada is dead. A chance arrow took his life from him. So Harold Godwinson was the winner after all.'

Hereward felt that he wanted to weep for his dead King; and wanted to curse Harold Godwinson in the same breath. The thin man patted him on the shoulder and said, 'I understand, comrade. Hardrada was my King also. As for Godwinson, the curse is already on him. He slew his own brother in the battle, and the Gods will never forgive that. Now his doom has started. A messenger came to him with ill tidings. Duke William has landed in the south. If Harold Godwinson rides ten horses to death he will not get to London in time to save his kingdom.'

Hereward cried out with pain suddenly, then said, 'What is wrong with me, friend?'

The thin man said, 'A cracked rib or two, no more, I would guess. A lord's horse fell on you. We should have left you for dead, but at his end Hardrada saw that you still breathed and commanded us to carry you to the ships.'

Hereward bit his lips to stop himself from crying out again. At last he said, 'We have lost the battle, and yet Godwinson has let us go back to the ships? That is strange, coming from such a man.'

'Godwinson gives nothing away. We came to England in three hundred ships; he is letting us take two dozen back to Norway. The profit is on his side. Yet, Odin knows, we have hardly enough men left to take even those ships back up to Bergen. The sea will claim most of us, I fear.'

Hereward was angry at these words, and began to say that his wife and son were waiting for him in Norway, and that he would reach them whatever the time of year, however deep the seas. But the thin man was groaning in his turn now, and almost fainting from the pain of his wounded arm.

Then at last they both began to laugh. 'Before Odin,' said Hereward, 'but we are a fine pair of warriors! To hear us, a man would say that we were two lads with toothache! Warriors, indeed!'

By the time they had done laughing they came over a wold and

79

looked down on the spot where the Ouse flows into the broad Humber. Now it was dusk, and the big river rolled as dull as lead on its way to the sea. Some gleams of moonlight came from behind the low autumn clouds and glinted on the slow waters. But there were no ships.

Hereward eased himself off the pony and stood panting for a while, searching for any sign of life below. At last he said, 'It seems that the two dozen ships have gone without us, friend. It seems that Olaf, the King's son, and Earl Paul of Orkney could not wait for their comrades before sailing.'

The thin man sank on to the grass, hugging his arm and moaning. 'If I had not stayed for you,' he said, 'I should have been with them, wherever they are. Curse on you, carle! You have lost me my home.'

Hereward said, 'I have neither sword nor helmet nor byrnie left, friend, or I would repay you with them. I am stripped as clean as the crow strips the young rabbit.'

The man spat on the ground and said, 'Curse your sword and your byrnie! You have lost me my freedom, man. Who can be stripped cleaner than that?'

Hereward saw that it was no use arguing with him any longer. Groaning with the effort, he struggled back on to the pony and said, 'I took you for a good friend. Now I see that I was mistaken, for you are a poor fellow. But there is nothing to be gained by quarrelling. Lie quiet and I will go and look for someone who might help you—there must be a leech or an old woman skilled in medicines down there by the river.'

He put the pony to a trot down the hillside, though every hoof-fall sent pain through his body. At last he could hear the thin man calling out no longer, nor could he see him, the dark had come down so heavily.

Hereward was in the middle of another fit of groaning at the pain his ribs were giving him when three men came from behind a gorse clump and stood in his way. The moonlight touched their helmets and spear-points. The harsh sound of their voices halted Hereward in his misery.

'Stay where you are, man,' said their leader. 'One more step and this spear is for you.'

Hereward began to laugh again wildly at these words, for he had recognized the accent of the man who threatened him.

'Danes!' he said. 'Danes come into England again! Does Swein the Crow think he can snatch up bigger titbits than Harald the Raven, then?'

The leader nodded and said, 'King Swein will do well enough, big-mouth! In this land now there will be pickings enough for any man who keeps his wits about him.'

Then, seeing that Hereward was in pain, he said, 'One of you lads lead the pony down to the camp and get the leech to look at this fellow. If we can mend him, he might be useful to us. He has something of the warrior-look about him.'

But before Hereward let the Danish doctor attend to him he insisted that someone should go back up the hill and bring down the northman with the wounded arm.

14. Gay Bargain

THE ARMY of Danes had come up the Humber into England, hoping to profit by the unsettled state of the country, trying to get a foothold in Yorkshire and especially in Lincolnshire, where their ancestors had lived in the old Danelaw many years before.

Hereward, weak with his wounds, his leader dead and without sword or money, stayed with them. As he rested in their tents, he heard news from other parts of England. He learned that Harold Godwinson had died on the hill at Hastings and, as Christmas came, that Duke William the Norman had been crowned at West Minster, after some sort of rioting.

But the Danes he was with were not greatly concerned with such matters. They were crafty men, who moved from place to place, living largely in moorland country, raiding villages here and there to get food, but generally keeping out of harm's way.

Up and down the land risings broke out, many of them at the instigation of the English Earl Waltheof, who claimed descent from one of the most ancient families of the north.

But then the news came to the Danes that even Waltheof, like the Prince Edgar the Atheling and the Earls Edwin and Morcar, had made friends with the new conqueror, and were travelling with him about England, to persuade the folk to lay down their arms at last. But wars were always flaring up, then dying down, like heath-fires, and one rumour often contradicted another. Some men said that William had gone home to Normandy; others said that his oldest friend, William fitz Osbern, ruled England now; still others claimed that Bishop Odo of Bayeux, the King's half-brother, was regent.

Hereward paid little heed to all this. His mind was set on getting over the sea to Norway as soon as he was well again, and finding his wife and son once more.

By now he was accepted among the Danes, who called him Badger, because of the grey streaks in his hair. As he grew stronger he took a number of them on at wrestling, and always won. So, in the end, they gave him a place at the headman's table and always consulted him before they went on a raid.

Then, one day, a small ship came into the Ouse near Riccall, and cloaked men stepped out of it.

One of them was King Swein himself. He saw Hereward

straightway and went to him, smiling strangely. 'Well,' he said, 'and so you know which man it is best to follow at last, my friend?'

Hereward stared at him for a while, then said, 'My true lord was killed under Landwaster. I have promised my sword to no man since.'

King Swein began to laugh and drew Hereward into the shelter of a wind-break. 'Come, come, friend,' he said. 'A man must be practical in this world. He must do the best for himself and his family.'

The way he said the last words made Hereward glance at him sharply. 'What do you mean?' he asked.

King Swein took a long time to answer; but at last he said, 'A man's family is always important to him—or should be. And not so long ago two folk came begging to my house—a lady named Euphemia and a little boy named Cnut. I took them in because the lad's name is one I am fond of.'

Suddenly Hereward's heart leaped with joy. He looked at King Swein with a new understanding.

'My wife and son are at your court, Swein?' he asked.

The Dane nodded. 'They are safe and sound there,' he said. 'And one day, before long, mayhap, they will be safe and sound in England. That is, if the head of their house will see good Danish sense and stop galloping through dreamland to find fairy gold!'

Hereward kneeled before King Swein and said, 'Lord, my only dream is of happiness with my kin. The only gold I desire is my dear wife and son. I am your man, if you will promise to return these two to me safely.'

King Swein smiled and nodded. 'I will keep you to that,' he said. 'Hereward, you are my man and I am your lord. May God send storm to sink my ships if I betray you after this. And may he send lightning to strike you down if you betray me. Is it a bargain?'

Hereward nodded dumbly.

'Very well,' said the Dane, after they had drunk a horn of beer together, 'I am not in England for pleasure. I am here to see how the land lies; and soon I shall come up the Humber with the banners flying. And, with God's help, I shall go to York and set up my standard there, as poor Hardrada once hoped to do.'

Hereward bowed his head and said, 'Do not ask me to go to York. I will not follow another leader into that fateful city.'

But King Swein said merrily, 'Say no more, old enemy! I have other plans for you. You shall stay here, or in Lindsey, or in the Isle of Axholme till I get to Denmark and back again. I shall not ask you to go north again to York. Your task will be to lead the men of Lindsey towards London when I return! They will follow you because you are one of them; your forefathers from the north-land once settled in Lincolnshire as theirs did, in the old Danelaw that they wrested from English Alfred. How does that seem, soldier? How would you like to lead these Englishmen who were once Danes?'

Hereward took the King's hand and said, 'It seems well, lord. Only bring my family to me, when you return.'

King Swein stood up, as a sign that his talk with Hereward was ended. He said, his right hand raised high, 'If I do not deliver them to you, then may I lose all I have gained. Will that suit you, thegn?'

Hereward bowed his head and said, 'No man could ask for more, lord.'

Then he went from the wind-break smiling so broadly that the other Danes nudged each other and smiled, thinking the English-man had taken leave of his senses.

15. The Man in the Marsh

THE TALL reeds stood about Hereward like watchers, whispering to each other in the night wind. All round him the waters of Ouse and Trent gurgled darkly at his feet, catching for a moment the reflections of scudding clouds and fitful moon-gleams. It was as though the sky lay at his feet, not above his head. And over his head, what? The rushes were too high for a man to see far across Axholme. It was a wild, flat, desolate waste, cut through with water-channels, the marshland that lay between great rivers at their meeting-place. It was the home not of decent peasants, but of men outside all law.

Hereward thought: 'No army could take Axholme. The men would stumble into waist-deep mud, the horses would break their legs in ditches. Here, a man who knew his way about by night need fear no one—except other lawless ones like himself.'

He found a moss-covered rock and sat on it, casting his line into the black water without any hope of taking a fish. He had come to this lonely spot to think, to get away from plotting and planning and the treachery of one man against another. He had come to think quietly of his wife and son, the only creatures in all the world for whom he had affection now.

'If Swein keeps his word,' Hereward thought, 'the time may not be far away when we shall be together. Perhaps in the Welsh hills, or even in far Ireland, there is a valley, a village, where we can start again, and where we can forget the men who struggle for a worthless crown or a wooden throne.'

As he was thinking this a water-rat slid into the puddle beside him with a hasty splash. Then a heron suddenly took to the wing beyond the reeds, crying harshly. The hair on Hereward's neck rose; if the wild creatures were disturbed, there must be a reason, he thought. His hand went down to his empty sword-belt, and then he remembered and smiled bitterly. His sword lay shattered on the field at Stamfordbridge. Unless, by now, some farmboy had refashioned it into a hedging-knife. Hereward shrugged his shoulders and, thinking what a poor weapon his fishing-rod would be, cast his line once more and decided that no man, not even a great king like Hardrada, could stay the hand of fate once it was clenched to strike.

He even began to whistle, a gay little love-song that was still going the rounds of the camps, though it was three generations old by now:

Come, sweetheart, come,
Dear as my heart to me,
Come to the room
I have made for thee.

Here there are couches spread,
Tapestry tented
Flowers for thee to tread,
Green herbs sweet-scented . . .

And as he whistled he thought of Euphemia; and he smiled in his heart, a little bitterly, to think of the couches and the flowers he could offer her now—a heap of damp hay under a wind-break and marsh-marigolds. No more!

Then, as he reached the end of the second verse, he heard the rushes part behind him, and was suddenly aware that someone stood looking down at him. The moonlight cast a long dark shadow at Hereward's feet, and he knew then that this must be a very big man.

He had begun to whistle the third verse when the man behind him said in a slow and thoughtful voice, 'An English fisherman whistling the *Iam, Dulcis Amica*. That is something I never hoped to hear.'

Hereward turned his head slowly and tried to get a sight of the man, but the moon stood behind the stranger and all Hereward saw was a burly, hunched figure in a heavy riding-cloak, and wearing a round iron helmet.

Hereward turned back and pretended to be busy with his line. 'Any man may whistle a love-song,' he said, 'whether he is English or not, whether he is fishing or not. Love is for all men, stranger.'

The cloaked man came beside Hereward and stood there silently for a while before saying, 'Aye, that is true—but how many men today think of love?'

Hereward heard the sword clanking beneath the long cloak. He guessed there would be a dagger too. He began to whistle again.

The man said, 'Have I your permission to sit beside you?'

Hereward moved over on the mossy rock and said, 'I do not own Axholme. You have as much right as I have, stranger.'

The man bowed his head and sat down. Then he eased back his heavy helmet with its nose-guard and spread his legs. He seemed a very confident man, one who could size up a situation quickly, one who knew no fear. He said quietly, 'I would say you were a man of sense—yet you come fishing here at midnight. Surely, no fish will bite now? And just as surely it is dangerous for an unarmed man to sit among the reeds where he cannot see who is coming at him?'

Hereward smiled and answered, 'I have eaten so much fish in Norway that I never wish to see a fish again. This rod is an excuse to give me something to hold in my hand. As for Axholme being dangerous, it is no more so than a ship on the winter sea, a meadow outside York, a room in a king's house, the high altar of a church. Men die in any place that God decrees. Death can reach a man although he builds walls as thick as those of Dover round him.'

For a while there was only the sound of the wind and the water and a night-hawk harrying the small marsh-fowl.

Then the man said, 'Have you a wife, friend?'

Hereward nodded. 'A lovely wife and a lusty son,' he said.

The man said gently, 'Then why do you not go to them, and keep clear of bloodshed?'

Hereward said, 'That is good advice. But my wife is in Norway, and I cannot swim as far as that until the weather gets better.'

The man laughed and said, 'I deserved that reply. My own wife is in Normandy. Though I am more fortunately placed in that I could go in my own ships to join her, whatever the season.'

Hereward said, 'Then why don't you go? Why sit talking in the mud to a fool like me when you could be happy?'

The man said, 'Can I try your rod and line? I have not fished since I was a lad. There has always been too much to do.'

Hereward handed him the rod and chewed a grass-stalk while the other cast the bait a time or two.

At last the man handed back the rod and said, 'This is not my lucky day, but it is yours.'

87

Hereward began to wrap the line round the rod, carefully, because he might need to use it tomorrow. Slowly he said, 'I do not consider it greatly fortunate to meet a stranger and to hear that his wife is in Normandy. That does not bring my own wife nearer to me. It does not put gold in my pouch.'

The cloaked man smiled and said, 'In my life, I have observed that it is the chance encounter that brings great things with it—not always the carefully planned meeting.'

He rose and stretched and yawned. His cloak parted and Hereward saw the long mail hauberk and the heavy chausses that reached down to the ankle. He saw the long sword and the broad-bladed dagger.

He said, 'You are a Norman from the camp in Lindsey. You are not so wise yourself to cross the Trent on a night as dark as this. I would advise you to go back before the dawn comes.'

The man said, 'I shall do that. But I am weary of knights and barons and priests. Weary of camp gossip. I thought I would visit my enemies for a spell; at least they want nothing from me, except my death.'

Hereward said, 'You seem to be a bit of a fool, like me.'

The man nodded. 'That is what I thought,' he said. 'I think we both had a Viking grandfather—and that always leaves a man a bit weak in the head.'

Hereward reached among his bundle of clothes on the ground and found his skin-bag of ale. 'Then let two stupid Vikings drink together,' he said. 'This is a drink that is brewed according to an old recipe from Acre.'

The man squirted the ale into his mouth so that it made a glistening arc in the moonlight. Now his head was back and his dark stubbled chin was thrust upwards. But he did not seem to think that he was in any danger.

He wiped his lips then handed back the goat-skin. 'It is flavoured with cinnamon and a touch of clove,' he said, thoughtfully. 'I like it—but I confess I am more at home with our own rough cider of Normandy. Come with me, friend, and we will drink it in Falaise together next summer under the oak trees in the sun.'

Hereward laughed and said, 'I have never been offered a holiday before on the strength of one draught of ale! You *must* be a fool, man!'

The other began to laugh, too, and said, 'I am not offering you a mere holiday, fisherman. I am offering you my friendship and perhaps a holding of land—enough to rear your son on, and keep your wife in new dresses and jewellery.'

Hereward stood, too, and looked more closely at the man. 'Friend,' he said, 'I think you are some homesick captain who needs a drinking-mate. Well, you'll find one, sooner or later, here or there, and then you'll be content. But don't go about the country promising everyone you meet a holding of land—or one day Duke William will get to hear about it, and then you'll have no ears left to keep your helmet on! Take my advice, soldier. That Duke of yours is not to be trifled with.'

The man laughed and said, 'He calls himself "King" now, have you not heard? Archbishop Aeldred put the crown on his head, and the Bishop of Coutances read out the ceremony in good French. It was all done according to law. Even Edith, the Confessor's widow, agreed to it.'

Hereward said bitterly, 'She is Godwinson's sister. So she has an eye to profit. Of course she would agree.'

The man said, 'You hated Harold then? I have found many hundreds who did—and only a few dozen who did not. That sort of king must always look to be hated, even by his own people. Yet who else was there? Only Edgar the Atheling, whose lips are scarcely dry of his mother's milk; and those two rogues, Edwin and Morcar, who would sell their dearest friend to keep what they have got.'

Hereward shook his head and said; 'Do not spoil a pleasant meeting by this talk of policy. Keep it for your camp, and the priests and barons there. All I want now is a quiet farm and a big dog outside the gate to keep away meddling captains who want me to shed my blood so that they can sit more securely on their stolen thrones.'

The big man put his hand on Hereward's shoulder. 'Friend,'

he said easily, 'what else does any man want? It is only that some men are called by destiny to sit on thrones and bring peace to the land. Ask any king, and you will find that all he wants, in his heart, is a quiet farm and that big dog outside the gate to keep meddlers away.'

Hereward could, if he had wished, have snatched the dagger from the man's belt just then, and have put it into his heart, through the opening under his armpit. But he said, 'What do we know of kings, stranger? Two fools standing in a bog at midnight, our senses fuddled with a draught of ale! Go on your way, friend, and good fortune keep you safe when the arrows whine again and the horses plunge.'

The man seemed a little sorry to part so abruptly. He held Hereward's arm a while and said, 'You may be a fool, but you are an honest fool. Come with me and I swear, by God's Splendour, that you shall have all your heart's desire in return for your honest fool's friendship.'

Hereward gently drew his arm away and said, 'There is only one man who swears by God's Splendour, friend—and that is your own Duke, William the Norman. Do not overreach yourself, using the Duke's oaths, and offering rewards to every landless man you meet; or one day you will find yourself in the dungeon at Falaise and no tongue to offer with! God go with you over the river. Good night.'

The man stood still in the moonlight, with the waters murmuring about him, as Hereward pushed his way through the rushes back to the staked causeway leading to the Danish camp.

He called softly to Hereward, 'Let me advise you, too, friend. Make your way from this place before tomorrow night. After that, you might wish you had accepted my offer.'

Hereward waved to him and said, 'Into your boat, Norman. You will get rheumatics standing there in the marsh. Only Englishmen and frogs can live in such places.'

The man was still standing there, watching him, when Hereward turned round. But though he waved, Hereward did not make any reply. He was thinking of Euphemia and Cnut once more.

Part Three

1068 - 1072

16. Black Bargain

TIME PASSED. In York, Englishmen rose and burned their own city, then butchered the Normans who came to suppress them. Great earls led the English rebels; men like Morcar and Waltheof, who looked like a lion with his mane of hair.

And then the Conqueror came north and put the villages to the torch, and men to the sword. Slaves in the north fetched no price at all. You could have bought a man for less than you could a horse or a cow. The countryside stank with smoke. Young children crept from house to house in the districts that escaped, begging to be put to some task in return for food to fill their swollen bellies. They were weary of eating acorns and grass.

The north had become a wilderness. It was even worse than when the Danes had come, in the time of Ethelred.

Hereward was at Brigg in Lindsey. There he ate well and had his feet to a warm fire. The men of Lindsey were old men of the Danelaw. They knew how to hide away a man who was wanted by the foreign soldiers. They knew how to keep their mouths shut—and their front doors open.

Hereward dined each day with the sons of Swein of Denmark, who had a shelter a little way up the street, beyond the church.

Each night, as the torches flared, they told him, 'When our father comes again into the Humber, all will be well with you. Give him your help, call the folk here about you to fight for him, lead them—and you shall have your wife and son again. Swein the King has promised this, and he is not the man to go back on his word. He is a Dane, my friend.'

Hereward bowed his head and smiled secretly. He, too, knew

93

Danes. And they were not always as they thought they were, in other men's eyes.

But the months passed and still there was no news of Swein setting forth from Denmark.

One bright morning Hereward went into the little square-towered church beside the River Ancholme and knelt before the plain altar there. In a low voice he said, 'God, I have been a laggard in observing Your wishes. That I acknowledge. I like a straight-speaking man, God. I like a man who admits to his faults, whether he be a cowherd or a thegn. I have been too full of other things, Lord. But now I have the sense to see that I have been wrong. Forgive me, God.'

Candles fluttered in the draughty little church, and women up for the market crossed themselves to see this big, raw-boned soldier, a sword and dagger beside him, muttering so loudly.

Hereward said, 'God, a bargain with You, if You please.'

He waited for a while, to see if the candles went out, or a sudden thunderstorm flung tiles from the church roof. But these things did not happen, so Hereward went on.

'God,' he said, 'I have a wife and a son, and to me they are more than anything in life. More than the sun in the sky and the corn in the earth. More than the fishes in the river, or the stars in the heavens.'

He waited once more, in case there was a sign. But there was only a small hunched weary priest who passed up and down to see that no boys stole the wax candles from the platform before the image of the Virgin; or no peasants, drunk in the market square, flung turfs through the windows, being northmen by blood and so not real Christians.

At last, when Hereward was sure that God was not angry with him, he said, 'Lord, this is my offer; bring my dear ones back to me and I will serve You, and see that You are served in this land, whatever the cost.'

His eyes strayed to his weapons, and his thoughts swung away a little.

'But, God,' he said sternly, as though talking to a troop of

94

soldiers, 'if You do not bring them back to me, then I will not answer for the rest. Is that agreed, God?'

For a while there was nothing different to be heard in the town. The doves cooed as always in the square, the river burbled on its way down from the Wolds to the great Humber, the solid wooden wheels of the farm wagons crunched over the cobbled streets of the town. Then, far away and faint, a sound came from the blue sky. It was a hawk's feeding-call. Up above the thatch and tiles of the little town the questing bird had seen a partridge skimming the walls and barns.

Now the hawk came down with a swish of pinions and a scream that grew louder and louder.

Nimble, the partridge swung into the church porch and the safety of the oaken stools and trestles. The hawk, unable to stay its furious course, struck the porch and fell gasping before the door. Hereward rose and went to see what had happened. The bird, dying, glanced at him out of a raging amber eye, its feathers twisted and broken, its claws clenching on nothing in its last agony.

Under the clerk's high desk, the fat partridge chirked and twittered with fear. Then seeing the hawk dead, it danced out on pudgy feet, feathers preened, and swept over the churchyard chittering a silly victory cry.

Hereward saw this, as he turned the dead bird over with his foot. And he wondered what it meant—whether he was the hawk or the partridge; whether God was the hawk. Whether this was God's answer.

The little snuffling priest stopped by him, his eyes red-rimmed, his nose needing wiping in the chill of the early northern spring.

'That was a fine bird, master,' said the priest.

Hereward nodded and said, 'It died for a prey that was hardly worth the taking, priest.'

The small man nodded, then said, 'Men are the same. They die for nothing. No one can stop a man from doing that. At Stamford-bridge, at Hastings, and now again at York, they die. Always they die.'

Hereward went back and fetched his sword and dagger. He buckled them on as he spoke to the priest.

'Is it not their affair?' he asked.

The priest smiled and crossed himself. 'Nothing is ever a man's affair simply, master,' he said. 'It is between a man and God. Yet some are so stupid that they think they can rule their lives without God's aid. And some are even more vicious—for they think they can strike a bargain with God, as they would with a farmer selling oats, or a fishwife down on the wharf with her baskets.'

Hereward said slowly, 'A man cannot make a bargain with God, you say, friend?'

The priest shook his head. His nose was very red in the wind that blew up from the Ancholme.

'Master,' he said, 'with God there are no bargains to be made. *Everything* belongs to God—so the man and what he bargains for both belong to God. How then may a man bargain for what is already God's? It is common sense, friend.'

Hereward wanted to say more to him, but the man had gone into the church again, to watch over the candles; and Hereward felt that it would be beneath his pride to follow him and ask for more reasons.

He went back to his lodging, somewhat troubled in mind. An hour later a carle came in the door and said, 'Strap on your sword, Hereward. Swein of Denmark is coming, and he holds you to your oath of fealty. You are his man. So you must aid him.'

Hereward said, 'What does Swein wish me to do, fellow?'

The carle smiled and answered, 'He wishes you to raise the good Danes of Lincolnshire and to lead them down to sack the Golden Borough. Swein will come up the Witham or the Ouse and meet you by the time you have collected the plunder.'

Hereward said, aghast, 'Sack the Golden Borough, carle? Sack Peterborough? That is a heathen act.'

The man began to pick his teeth with a thorn and said, 'Such words mean nothing to me. Heathen—Christian—Muslim . . . I have heard them all. And I have fought for and against them all.

96

There is no virtue, or vice, in that. All over the world men are fighting "for God", they say. At various times, all win, and all lose. The corpse that fought for Allah is as dead as the one that fought for Christ.'

Hereward remembered his prayer in the little church that day, and he said, 'Nay, I'll not have that, carle. A true Christian goes to Heaven—that's the difference.'

But the carle went on picking his teeth, and only said, 'I have fought with Muslims who say they will go to Paradise. I have an uncle at Hedeby who still thinks he will end up at Odin's table in Valhalla. The little priest down the road at the church will tell you that a warrior goes to Heaven. It seems to me that the reward is the same—just as the death is the same. Nay, thegn, what seems to matter most is not the death or the after-death—but the pickings, while a man is alive and standing on his two feet. That is why you should sack the Golden Borough, for there is more wealth, good golden wealth, there than a man could find outside Miklagard. Get to it, thegn, and do not be late when Swein comes.'

17. The Golden Borough

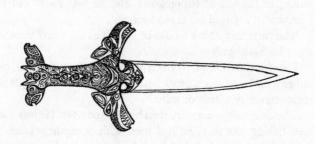

So, WITH great misgivings, Hereward gathered about him a swarming army of Lindsey men, folk who spoke Danish before

97

English, folk who hated Saxons almost as much as Normans. Between Brigg and Grantham he collected two thousand landless men with swords and spears, and together they went down the wooded roads towards Peterborough, each with the dream of plunder and of a fortune in his head.

Hereward did not dream of gold; he dreamed of the different reward that Swein would bring him—of Euphemia and his son. For those two he would have sacked the West Minster, let alone Peterborough.

As the men marched down, often by night, they told each other that they were not acting evilly; that the five great abbeys of Peterborough, Thorney, Crowland, Ramsey, and Ely were in the hands of the devil, and should be freed. It was different, they argued, when Abbot Brand held Peterborough—for Brand spoke Danish and held for the old Danish kings. But Brand was dead now, and William had appointed a foreigner to look after the Golden Borough. This was Thorold of Fécamp, who had come up from Malmesbury to take control, and who was more of a bloody knight than a churchman.

By the end of May, Hereward's untidy army was within sight of the fenland. Looking across the marshy wastes to where the tall tower of Peterborough rose, Hereward said to his chief carle, 'When I was a lad, my old father held lands here. Old Abbot Ulfketil of Crowland assigned some of the Abbey's estate to my father, in the vill of Rippingdale. But he was burnt out when Harthacnut avenged his tax-collectors.'

The carle said, 'Now would be as well as any other time to get them back, thegn.'

Hereward answered, 'If the truth be told, there may still be my father's name on documents here. I might still have a claim on some stretch of marsh or mire.'

The carle laughed and rubbed his hooked nose. He was used to men talking like this; he had been with common soldiers who swore that their fathers had been kings in Ireland, or among the Icelanders.

He said, 'I shall believe this when I see it.'

And Hereward, almost as a jest, replied, 'And see it you shall, fat one!'

That night, as the army lay under hedges and in ditches, not daring to light fires lest they were seen, a ragged man with a sparse greyish beard came through the reeds and asked for Hereward. And when he stood before Hereward he said, 'I come from King Swein. He has sent his ships a different way after all; up the Ouse to Ely. From there he will come in small smacks along the Nene to Peterborough, and will be there by midday tomorrow to take the Abbey. If you are there to share it, good; if not, still good, for then Swein will have all the more for himself, and none to share it.'

Hereward said, 'Tell Swein that I will be there at midday tomorrow. And tell him that it is not gold or silver I come for, but the other reward he promised me—my wife and son. Tell him that.'

After he had drunk mead and had eaten barley bread, the man went off along the ditches as silently as a marsh-adder.

Hereward could hardly sleep that night for thinking of his wife and son. In the morning he was up before any of his men and was armed in his iron helmet and byrnie. As he prowled among the reeds and ditches he tried to remember what Euphemia's voice had sounded like; but it was too much for him and he gave it up, lest he should begin to cry before the men.

By midday the army had reached the Golden Borough, some of them walking up to the waist in ditches, others knee-deep in the slime of the marshes.

All was so still that to Hereward it seemed God was watching all he did. He passed the word round among his soldiers that they were not to deal too harshly with the monks; but only to lay on if they came against Norman knights or footmen. The men of Lindsey smiled and nodded, and then forgot what he had said, as though the wind that blew across the marsh had taken their minds with it.

No Normans guarded the long low-roofed monastery which lay before the Abbey. And when Hereward blew on his horn and the rush started, only monks in their hampering robes appeared, holding up crosses and shouting prayers as though they were beset by heathens.

Hereward called out to them that all was well, and that no harm was meant to them. But the monks were so afraid of the Lindsey men with their knives and axes that they turned and ran howling in all directions like women, or hens when a fox is in the roost.

One of them, an oxlike man who had been a knight before he came to the Church, rolled up his sleeves and, taking up a log of firewood, struck down three of Hereward's men. This was the start of a terrible thing. Soon the Lindsey men were hitting out wherever they saw a monk, and soon they were inside the monastery, breaking open coffers and tearing down hangings and relics. But little enough they found there, for the monks had taken the precaution of carrying as much as they could inside the Abbey Church, which had great doors of oak.

While Hereward was trying to calm his followers, the prior of the place, Ethelwold, ran out and took him by the arm.

'For the love of God,' said the prior, 'is this the way to carry on? You are no better than the first Danes who brought such terror to the land.'

While he was speaking a party of rough men from Axholme broke down the Abbey doors and began to shout with joy at what they saw stacked up inside. Some of them came out with chests of gold and silver, some with holy garments, and some with jewelled shrines. Hereward got to the door in time to beat off a party of young men who were trying to tear down the great rood cross.

Prior Ethelwold was in tears, and only when Hereward told him that his own father had once held rights on lands at Crowland, and that, God willing, he would see that all was well, did the prior stop his lamentations.

Shortly after midday, flames rose up from the houses about the Abbey; and by sunset there was not a dwelling left whole in Peterborough.

Hereward walked alone, wondering what to do now, praying

silently that God would give him the chance to make good this destruction.

As the sun began to set over the flat marshland the Danish smacks and the rafts came up along the Nene, the men on them laughing loudly to see the smoke rising from the stricken town.

Hereward ran down to meet them. But Swein was not there, and the captain pushed Hereward aside and called out to the Lindsey men, 'Right, my comrades, bring the stuff aboard. We will all be off to Ely, where the King stays, and take the news to him. He will see to your rewards.'

Prior Ethelwold came to Hereward and said, tears on his cheeks, 'You have betrayed me and God, thegn. You said no harm should befall—yet my monks lie stark in the streets, the houses are all burned, and the treasures of the Borough are being taken away from the place. How will you answer that?'

Hereward shook his head sadly and said, 'Father, I had rather have lost my sword-hand than that this should have happened. Believe me, it was none of my wishing. Yet there is this consolation, that between the two of us, you and I, we may still get back some of God's treasures for the Abbey. And that we should never do if William of Normandy had laid hands on it—for he would have sent it straight to London.'

Together, Hereward and the prior boarded a raft and went along the Nene with the stacked treasures of the Borough, knee-deep in chalices and vestments, and holding tightly to all the images they could, so that these things did not slip into the muddy waters and be lost among the reeds for ever.

'If only I could recover the arm of the blessed St Oswald, that would be something,' wept the prior. 'It lay in a reliquary near the rood cross. I should know the coffer if I ever saw it again, I am sure.'

By now Hereward was too full of his own grief.

'Keep searching, father,' he said. 'Keep searching, and you are bound to find it. As I shall hope to find my family.'

This only seemed to make the prior weep all the more.

18. The Fortress at Ely

THAT EVENING Hereward stood in the presence of Swein of Denmark, in a barn on the Isle of Ely, a bare black place, with only a smouldering hearth-fire and a few rough stools to sit on.

Swein was with his sons, counting money from the Abbey coffers.

Hereward stood before him and said, 'I have done as you asked, God forgive me; now where are my wife and son, Swein?'

Swein looked up at him as though he could not see Hereward very well, as though he hardly existed. Then he said with a smile that showed his teeth, 'Would you leave a precious jewel on the roadside, man?'

Hereward looked puzzled and then said, 'No, King. Why do you ask?'

Swein smiled at one of his sons and answered, 'Yet you would have me bring your precious wife and son out among lawless men into the marshes. Does that make sense?'

Hereward did not know what to answer. Swein had him in a cleft stick. At last he said, 'I have waited long to see them, King. I thought you would stand by your bargain.'

King Swein rose and put on a very stern face. 'In the presence of my sons,' he said, 'are you accusing me of trickery, Hereward?'

Hereward hardly knew what to say, but he shook his head, although in his heart he mistrusted the Dane.

King Swein smiled and said, 'When a man sells a pig to another, does he expect payment that very day? Or, if he is a sensible fellow, might he not be prepared to wait one more week, and receive not only his payment, but the everlasting goodwill of his fellow?'

Hereward did not try to answer this, but instead turned from the King and said, 'I shall walk about the Isle and see what fortifications you have built. As for my share of the plunder, it is my wish that it be returned to the Abbey.'

King Swein bowed his head until Hereward had gone from the barn, and then he said to a servant, 'If ever there was a fool in England, that man is one. How he has lived so long and not learned more sense, I do not know!'

Then he and his sons went back to counting their treasures. And a while later, when the Prior Ethelwold broke in and weepingly demanded the holy relic of St Oswald, Swein turned to him carelessly and said, 'Aye, you shall have it, fellow. And if you are a quiet mouse of a man for another hour, you shall also be a bishop in my kingdom of Denmark. Now be off with you and let me count my gains.'

Ethelwold went in search of Hereward to tell him this, but he could not find the thegn.

Indeed, few men could have found him, for he was lying in a ditch, sighting along it and deciding where best to lay a stockade. In his loneliness, he had set his mind to fortifying the Isle of Ely as well as it could be done, against the time when William the Norman came up to seek his revenge for the attack on the Golden Borough.

The Isle was hardly more than a great mound of solid earth set among waving miles of rush and marshland. All about it water lapped in ditches and channels. Huge flocks of swamp birds lived there, and water-rats by the thousand. At night, in the moonlight, thick grey mists lay heavily over that deserted place. Stumps of rotting trees stood everywhere, relics of a time when forests grew there, now blackened and twisted wrecks, from which hung deep green mosses. No man, unless thief or outlaw, would wish to live in such a place. It was an island of sickening smells, of half-rotted vegetation, of strange night-noises, and of despair.

Yet there was this consolation, thought Hereward, as he moved from spot to spot, working out where a causeway should be built or a turf wall raised, no horse and no armed man could survive in this morass; only men who came on boats or rafts could reach the island—and they would be seen long before they got within striking range.

19. Departure and Attack

MEN WERE working everywhere among the reeds. The June sun caused their clothes to stick to their backs, and after a while, as they knocked in stakes, set up walls of turf, or made pit-falls, the men stripped off their shirts and worked, half-naked, to defend the Isle.

Hereward worked with the Englishmen, digging deep as anyone; dragging great bundles of faggots to build stockades, or willow-hurdles that would form the base on which mud roads might be made.

He met King Swein under a clump of damp alders. The Dane was sitting in the crook of a tree, gazing at his image in the water. He hardly noticed Hereward until the Englishman stood above him and their pictures mingled in the shimmering green pool.

Then Swein turned and said, 'Our men are building something that will serve a useful purpose, friend.'

Hereward nodded and asked when he would see Euphemia and Cnut.

The Danish king smiled and answered, 'Patience, man, patience. I have something more pressing to speak of. Your English prior, Ethelwold, has been behaving most oddly. Twice we have caught him in the barn, kneeling beside the coffers and praying. And three times we have come on him with a hammer and chisel in his hands. It is not like a priest to use such things, is it?'

Hereward said, 'As I am not a priest, I do not know what a priest is likely to do, Swein. But if you fear that poor Ethelwold means to rob you of your hoard, then set your mind at rest. He could not carry away all you have stolen!'

Swein glanced up furiously and said, 'Stolen? That was not stolen, man. I had William's permission to take it.'

Then, his sudden anger gone, he stared at Hereward like a boy caught stealing apples.

Hereward said softly, 'You are as straight as a hawthorn bough. You are as trustworthy as a moor-viper. Swein of Denmark, there are no men near us to hear, so we can forget who is the king and who the thegn—and I can tell you to your face that you are no comrade of mine from this hour on. When did you speak with the Norman? When did his messengers come to you? Why was I not told?'

King Swein began to whistle and hum, and to walk round the alder tree so as to put it between Hereward and himself.

He said at length, 'In statecraft a man has to make many decisions without noising them abroad. When kings speak to one another, must they do it in the town square, where every rogue and beggar may listen to them?'

Hereward took up a thick faggot of wood and snapped it over his bent knee. And when Swein left him he went to the alder tree and kicked it again and again in his rage.

'Swein of Denmark, you treacherous hound!' he was still saying, when he felt a light touch on his shoulder. Prior Ethelwold stood there, his face pale and frightened.

'My son,' he said, 'forgive me for disturbing you in your—devotions; but there is something I wish to tell you.'

Hereward turned, gazing at him as though he had never seen him before. 'What is it?'

The prior said gently, 'I do not know whether I have sinned or not; but I have been in the King's barn and have found the blessed arm of St Oswald and certain other relics.'

Hereward smiled then and said, 'Well, father, that is not so terrible, is it? That is what you wanted.'

The prior placed his hands together in the motion of prayer before he answered. 'I have sent them secretly to the Abbey at

Ramsey for safe keeping away from the Danes. . . . And I borrowed some of your Englishmen and one of your boats to do it.'

Hereward began to laugh at the good man's simplicity. Then he said, 'Well done, Ethelwold. Do you make me your accomplice in stealing from the Danish king relics which he had no right to?'

The prior looked at him like an owl and said, 'I always heard that you were a fierce man, who stood by his comrade, whether Christian or pagan, in all things. I expected to be beaten, or even hanged, for what I have done.'

Hereward was searching the marshes with his eyes. Suddenly he pointed and said, 'Look over there, Ethelwold. An adder is about to have a fat frog for his dinner. There, in the clump of dry reeds.'

The prior did not look, but took Hereward by the arm and said urgently, 'My son, in your opinion, did I do wrong? After all, King Swein treated me well, and promised me a bishopric if I ever wanted one.'

Hereward swung on him and said, 'Swein would promise you the moon and the stars, if he wished to use you for his own ends, father. He has used me, I fear—and now he has been in touch with William the Norman, who has made him a present of all the treasures of your Golden Borough.'

The prior sat on the damp ground as though he had been hit on the head with a staff, and said, 'I do not understand. What would William wish to gain by that, my son? What has Swein to give in return?'

Hereward said slowly, 'Nothing to give, father; but plenty to take away. With Danes, the taking-away is sometimes of more value than the giving.'

Prior Ethelwold looked up and said, 'This is a riddle to me, and I was never good at riddles. What does it mean?'

Hereward answered, looking over the darkening marsh, 'Swein has agreed to take away his armies and his ships out of England. That is of more value to William than if he stayed and fought alongside the English, is it not?'

The prior gasped and said, 'And the price William has paid for such treachery is our treasure—*our* treasure?'

Hereward nodded, and the monk got up and wandered away among the ditches, saying, 'I cannot believe it! No. I cannot believe it.'

But three days later he did believe it, when he woke to pray at dawn and saw the last of the Danish smacks and rafts moving laden along the wind-ruffled waterways, away from Ely.

The prior ran as fast as he could to the wind-break where Hereward slept with other English captains and wakened him.

'My son,' he said, 'the Danes have gone, just as you said.'

Hereward rubbed the sleep from his eyes and smiled. 'Yes, father,' he answered. 'I was up half the night, behind a rock, watching them make ready. This is no surprise to me, but I did think that Swein would have had the good neighbourliness to wish me farewell.'

The prior sat down beside him and smiled at last. 'Well,' he said, 'saving your presence, I will say what I have always said when Danes have gone: "Good riddance to bad rubbish!" '

Hereward looked at him strangely, then said, 'I counsel you to go back to Peterborough, father, and lock yourself in. I hear that your abbot, Thorold the Norman, is back again. You will be safe with him.'

The prior said, 'Safe? Safe from what, my son? Am I not safe here?'

Hereward rolled over as though he meant to sleep again and said, 'Do as I say, friend. There is nothing to be gained by staying on this island among lawless men. I will give you boats and rowers to take you back to where you belong. Make ready, father, and God go with you.'

The prior went away, puzzled, until later in the day a dark-faced man wearing a mail shirt down to his knees and a pointed helmet came off a boat and strode into the camp, carrying no weapons. In a proud Norman voice he said, 'To Hereward, and to all his captains, I bring the King's word. And this is what William of Normandy and England says to you: "Go now, lay down your arms, kneel before your nearest baron and swear to mend your ways." '

Hereward, who was sitting on a tree-stump eating a piece of salt pork, smiled and said to the man, 'That was a short speech to come all this way from a king. He could have written it on a parchment and put it in a flask. Then it would have floated along the streams to us one day. So you would have been saved the journey.'

The Norman knight pushed his helmet back, for it was uncomfortable in the sunshine. Then he said, 'William's speeches are all short. He speaks better with a sword than with words. As for that flask—it would have taken too long, and time is short. As for saving me the journey, I have not come very far. The King's army is stationed only ten miles from here. I thought your spies would have told you that, Hereward.'

Hereward flung the pork bone away, and said, 'No, I did not know. Last night it was the turn of the Danes to keep watch, and they left without telling me what they saw.'

The Norman looked round and said, 'Is there anyone with a jug of ale? It is a thirsty journey to get here, dressed in this harness, I can tell you.'

Someone brought the man a drink, and he sat down in the dirt beside Hereward, without asking permission, with his helmet off and his mail shirt unbuckled.

He was a merry fellow from Dol, red-faced and dark-haired, with two fingers missing from his sword hand. This made it hard for him to hold the ale-cup. But he did not seem to mind spilling the liquid on to his leather tunic. Like most of his folk, he came from the north and was rough and ready.

Hereward said to him, 'And what if I do not leave this place?'

'William did not tell me that. I suppose he thought you would do as he said, without question. Everyone else does.'

Hereward said again, 'What if we do not leave this place, friend?'

The knight stood up and handed the ale-cup to the man who had brought it to him. 'Well, then,' he said, 'I think that William will come and burn you out—that is, if this damp reed *will* burn! But if I were you, thegn, I would do just as the King says. There is little sense in standing before a hurricane or a flood, or any other Act of God.'

Hereward smiled and asked, 'So you think of your King as an Act of God, do you, knight?'

The man shrugged his shoulders and smiled. 'Of God, or the other one, it matters little; the end is the same!'

Hereward said in mock sternness, 'It is well for you that Prior Ethelwold has gone back to Peterborough. He would not allow such heathen talk!'

The knight put on his helmet again and buckled up his mail shirt. 'Thegn,' he said, 'you and I are soldiers, men of the earth. We know that what is to be will be. If a battle is won, it is won; and if a battle is lost, well, it is lost. No man can undo what has happened.'

Hereward said grimly, 'This battle is not lost, my friend. Not yet; no, not yet.'

The knight went away to his boat quite merrily, stopping every now and then to wave his hand at the Englishmen who worked among the rushes, knocking stakes into the mud, on which they would lay planks to complete a causeway and join the island to the rest of the marsh.

When he had almost disappeared Hereward called out to the men about him, 'Well, you have heard King William's word. He is coming to burn us out if we do not disperse. Many of you have homes and families. It is hard for any man to bear the loss of them. So, here and now, before all witnesses, I pledge my word that any of you who wish to leave Ely may do so, without hindrance, and without hard feelings from me. I have a strange desire to stay, to see what I can gain before I meet my family again. But none of you men need stay.'

He waited a long time, but no one spoke. The Englishmen stood about him, as still as statues in a church. Not one asked to go home.

Then a man with a hammer in his hand said, 'Thegn, we have

work to do. The last length of causeway to lay between ourselves and the marsh. Let us be about it!'

Hereward smiled and shook his head. 'No, friend,' he said. 'Let us leave a gap there for the time being. One day, we might come to bless that stretch of water—who knows? In the meantime, we have our boats and rafts. Let us be content.'

The men shrugged their shoulders and grinned at each other, but Hereward only smiled and then went away.

'Captains!' said the man with the hammer. 'I think they are all madmen!'

No one disagreed with him.

20. The Ruined Causeway

THE YEAR which followed began in glory and ended in utter ruin and despair.

A fortnight after the knight had brought William's warning five boatloads of Normans came up the waterways at dawn. But the English were awake this time, and had learned to move about the marsh with boards on their feet, like silent frogs. At a dark bend in the channel a group of them risked death by leaping from the rushes and staving in the enemy boats with pick-axes. Then, while the heavily-armed Normans floundered in the mud and slime, other Englishmen picked them off with long-headed arrows that could pierce mail shirts.

Only three Englishmen were lost that time, but at least forty Normans lay dead among the rushes, some of them sunk so deep into the marsh that they could not be stripped of their mail and swords.

Hereward smiled grimly over his ale that night, but said, 'Let us not think we have won yet, friends. The Norman is not a man to take such a reverse easily. He will be back before long to try again.'

By noon the next day, when the sun was almost overhead and some of the English were lying about, wiping their brows and playing chess, singing or betting against each other at the game of knuckle-bones, a hail of arrows fell into the camp, doing no harm, but carrying a further threat. Hereward, who was sitting in a tree, called down, 'They have come along our unfinished causeway—about three hundred of them, all on foot. Poor devils, they must think that we did not know of their arrival. Yet the spies have been passing back the curlew call for an hour or more.'

A thegn from Riseholme, near Lincoln, called back to him, 'Blow the horn then, and let our good fellows close in from the marsh.'

But Hereward shook his head. 'There is another plan,' he said. 'When the horn is blown, no one will close in. We shall sit in the sun, as we do now, and the Normans will perish without your aid!'

The thegn from Riseholme laughed and said, 'Very well, Hereward, blow it and let us see what happens.'

So Hereward put the horn to his lips, as another arrow flight whirred harmlessly through the air, and blew three long blasts.

The watching English on the island saw that far away the marsh seemed to come alive with men—men with great hammers and baulks of wood. Some of the Normans saw this, too, but they were too late and too far away to prevent what was to happen. The sound of hammers on wood came clearly through the summer air; then came the wrenching and groaning of timber. Suddenly a long piece of the causeway behind the Normans swayed on its pillars, went over, and sank into the sluggish ooze. The three hundred Normans were left standing on a lonely wooden platform, cut off from land at both ends.

An Englishman came slopping up out of the swamp, the ash boards still strapped on his feet, and said, 'What now, Hereward? Are the lads to tumble them down or to fill them with arrows?'

Hereward climbed out of the tree and said, 'Nay, Gurth, we will let God's sun and their armour kill them. Fetch the marsh-otters in and let them break their fast. They have carried out their work well.'

All that day the Normans stood on the length of broken causeway, cursing and shooting arrows. In the heat of the afternoon, many of them stripped off their mail and some of them even flung it into the marsh, in fury.

At least five of them tried to swim to solid ground, but they either drowned, or were pole-axed by Englishmen in the reeds.

The rest kneeled to pray, or shouted at the top of their voices for someone to come to their aid.

Hereward sat alone, wondering what should be done. At any other time he would have been ruthless in destroying his enemy. But, as he sat by the fireside in the barn that had been King Swein's, the voice of Euphemia seemed to come to him, saying, 'Have mercy, husband. Have such mercy on these poor devils as you would wish God to have on you, my love.'

When he could bear his thoughts no longer Hereward rose and went into the dusk to find his captains. One of them was the thegn of Riseholme, who had called up to him earlier when he sat in the tree. Hereward said to them, 'This is not God's will, my brothers. We cannot let these men starve out there. To kill swiftly in the heat of battle is one thing; but to stand by while men go mad in the night mist is another. We will push rafts out to them and let them make their own way back to their camp, if God wills it so. Get rafts, my friends.'

The thegn of Riseholme drew his sword and stuck it in the

marshy ground between himself and Hereward.

'Lord,' he said, 'here we are all free men. Most of us come from the old Danelaw, and we are not slaves to be sent running this way and that, at the master's will.'

Hereward looked down at the thegn's sword and said, 'This I know; why do you tell me, Thorkell? And why do you set your sword before me so? It is not a very fine weapon, and I have seen it before.'

Thorkell dragged his sword from the mud and said, 'It is not fine, but fine enough. You have seen it before, but you may never see it again—though you may well feel it.'

Hereward said, 'All my life I have lived among northmen. I know their ways, friend. And sometimes I become so weary of their trick of speech that I would sooner listen to jays chattering, pigs chuntering, oxen bellowing. Yes, friend, I would sooner listen to William and his prinking Norman tongue, at times. . . .'

Thorkell said angrily, 'Or your wife and her snarling Greek, I'd guess.'

Before Hereward knew what he was doing, he had made a fist out of his great right hand and thumped that fist into Thorkell's neck, just over his neck-ring.

The thegn's sword flew out of his hand into the marsh. Thorkell fell on his knees, gasping and holding his neck.

None of the other captains moved, for each knew that Hereward had done right to act as he did.

Hereward stooped and helped Thorkell up again. 'I am not sorry, brother,' he said, 'for you deserved to be reminded that I am your chosen leader. I am only sad that you should stick against me like that. Tomorrow I will see that you have another sword. Now get the rafts and let us give these Norman dogs a chance to live.'

But suddenly, in the dark, there came a deep groaning of wood, then a crunching, then a number of splashes. Men were shouting from the mist in foreign voices.

Thorkell smiled and said, 'God has answered us. The causeway has collapsed under their weight and they are drowning. Am I still to get out rafts, Hereward?' Hereward nodded, sterner than ever.

The Englishmen paddled out on rafts to where the causeway had stood. But now all was silent, and only the scared moorhens clucked in the dark.

The timbers of the causeway jutted up crazily like the fingers of a black giant in the milk-white mist. Perched on one splintered baulk was a Norman helmet, slung there by its owner when the sun had been too strong for him. It looked foolish and lonely and Hereward took a staff and knocked it off into the water. His face was a mask with no mouth.

In the morning his men went out and got back nearly two hundred swords and mail-shirts.

After this, Thorkell never crossed his leader again. He was killed early in August by the bite of an adder, when he was feeling under a clump of dry sedges for a plover's egg. Hereward was the last man he saw, and as the leader bent over him to wipe his sweating brow, Thorkell said, 'That blow you gave me, Hereward—I can still feel it! Here, in my neck. You are not a man I would wish to swap buffets with, you old rogue!'

Then he died, and Hereward was more sorry than he had been for the loss of a battle-mate since Hardrada fell under Landwaster.

21. The New Enemy

THE YEAR limped slowly enough among the rushes and the stinking water. Men's clothes wore out and they had to catch what creatures they could to keep themselves from nakedness—rabbits, hares, otters, and wild cats. They laughed to see each other dressed so like savages.

And they laughed again when they heard that the midland harvests had failed and that famine was making havoc among the

Norman garrisons. One night Hereward and a dozen picked men made their way into the outskirts of Cambridge, where William had set up his place, and there they heard that his common foot-soldiers were eating cats and dogs in some villages. In at least one manor the baron had begun to kill horses to feed his own family.

Hereward and his company journeyed the fifteen miles back to Ely in fine fettle. On the way they passed an old hedge-priest who said to them, 'Why are you laughing? Have you not heard that you and your ruffians are all excommunicated?'

Hereward flung the old man a silver penny and said, 'We'll meet Hell when the time comes; William is savouring Hell now!'

The old man shouted after them, 'You will be down to eating marsh-rats before the winter is over, my fine friends!'

But they gave no listening to him, for the Cambridge ale was still talking in their heads.

And when they reached the barn there was other news to make them merry. A sailor had come from the coast and brought news that King Swein had not done so well out of his double dealing after all. He had lost most of his ships in a storm, and what treasure he did land in Denmark had been largely burnt in a fire, when his guards had got drunk and careless.

Hereward laughed and told his men that God was clearly on the side of the English. And for a while it did seem that all might go well with the men of Ely—for almost every day rebel English folk joined them, until it became a common sight to see fresh followers breasting the reeds, waving rags on sticks, and calling out that they were friends.

But as time went on food became very scarce, and then Hereward began to think of what the old hedge-priest had said about the marsh-rats.

By October, winds as cold as a dead man's feet began to move across the fens, and many men who came from drier parts went down with rheumatics, or a sort of blindness that came from the seeds of the dry grasses carried on the breeze. Others caught a disease of the stomach, which some said came from the mists and others from the green water they drank.

In November, Earl Morcar came by night to join Hereward. He was dressed in black, and looked more like a beggar than the great lord who had once jested with kings.

In Hereward's barn Earl Morcar told how he and his brother, Edwin, had left William's court secretly; and how Edwin had gone on northwards, hoping to get help from Scotch Malcolm against the Normans. At this point he stopped in his story, and Hereward prompted him, 'What then, friend?'

Morcar drew with his finger on the table-top, making the shape of a head. He said slowly, 'Those who rode with him turned on him beside some river. Cursed be the name of the place! My brother fought well, but they pulled him off his horse and then took his head to show William. May they be for ever cursed!'

Hereward put his hand on the Earl's shoulder and said, 'One day, friend, we will get revenge for him.'

But Morcar shook his head. 'Sometimes,' he said, 'I think that William is the devil himself. Sometimes, I think that no man will ever best him.'

Hereward laughed. 'Be of good heart, comrade! We will see what we can do when we have our army drilled and well fed again.'

Then winter struck in all truth. The men of Ely woke one morning to find that their world had turned to white, and that all the waterways were frozen. The ice was so thick that it would have borne men on horses.

Hereward was distressed at this, for in such weather the Normans could come on foot, without aid of boats or bridges, and attack the stronghold.

He sent out scouts, who fixed mutton-bones on their feet and used them as skates, to see what was happening. But all the news they brought was that the King had placed uncounted ships along the Great Ouse and the Little Ouse, and that he had more soldiers than men had ever seen before in that part.

Then a new problem arose. Starving peasants began to come to Ely; men who had never held a sword in their lives. They came begging for food and saying that they had been turned from their homes by the soldiers and that Hereward owed them life.

Against their will, Hereward and Morcar set men on to drive back the peasants with staves and many on both sides were killed as they wrestled in the frozen waters. And the time came when Hereward went to the monks of Ely and said, 'This I hate to do—to beg for food from you, I, under a curse for sacking the Golden Borough.'

The abbot, Thurston, looked at him with small red-rimmed eyes and said, 'My son, our own larders are empty and we live on scraps of old boiled leather and the bark of trees. We can only pray for you. Let us hope God listens.'

And when Hereward had gone back to his fortress the abbot smiled and sent a fast messenger into Cambridge to tell King William that the time was almost ripe now.

22. The New Causeway

BY CHRISTMAS Hereward's case was a severe one. In the harsh winter many of his men died, and many others made their way by night northwards, hoping to reach the deserts of Yorkshire, where they might gain a living as robbers, away from the garrisoned towns.

The bells of Ely echoed across a scene of desolation. All was white or black, snow or rotting reeds. Hereward sat with Morcar in the tumbledown barn, rubbing his hands to keep life in them.

Morcar said, 'Life is strange, friend. There was a time, when you were with Hardrada, that I thought you were a fiend, a wolf that should be killed out of hand. Now I love you like my own brother, like Edwin who is stark.'

Hereward said, 'In my life I have loved only a few—and always I have lost them, this way or that. It seems to me that love is a weakening emotion. To love is to strip off

the mesh-shirt and stand bare to the sword-thrusts of fate.'
Morcar listened to the bells for a while, then answered, 'Yet
what is life for, if we are to deny love? I, who have been a great
lord, almost a king, once had palaces and jewels, tasty foods and
wines, soft beds, music in my halls, lords as my slaves. But now
I have nothing; only a stool to sit on, and a threadbare cloak which
would not keep out the smallest breeze. What does all this mean,
if I am not to love either? Why are we on earth, Hereward?'

Hereward was feeling the rheumatics starting in his right arm
and leg, and his belly was empty. He spoke sharp and said, 'Do you
think I am God, to answer such questions? Have I not sorrows
enough, without your mewling day and night?'

Afterwards he was sorry he had spoken so, and went walking
among the icy meres, wondering how he could make his peace
with Morcar again.

In a small hollow he came on the rotting carcass of a sheep. It
lay with its fore- and hind-legs bound with cord, as though someone had been carrying it to a feast.

He wondered what had happened to the carriers. He found
them, lying huddled together in a ditch, less than ten paces from
the carcass. They were fisher-folk, by their dress, and their faces
were black with plague. How long they had lain there, he could not
guess; but long enough for their burden to rot, even in such cold
weather.

Hereward stepped quickly back to the barn where Morcar still
brooded, and said, 'Brother, it is finished. We cannot last any
longer here.'

He told Morcar what he had seen out by the mere. But the
Earl hardly seemed to grasp what was said. He only stared at
Hereward as though he had seen a ghost.

That night Hereward led him out across the marsh towards the
village of Aldreth, where the Ouse was crossed by an ancient
causeway and there were the ruins of an old church that men said
the Romans had set up before even the Danes came.

Two score men went with them, leaving the mound and the
barn deserted.

Morcar said, 'I would to God that William would put us out of our misery, for our luck has dwindled day by day until it seems that the end must be near.'

Hereward answered, 'Have courage, brother. The Normans will not expect us to be here. They will look for us elsewhere. And in the meantime we can hunt a little, rob a little, fast a little, until the spring comes.'

Morcar laughed mirthlessly at these words, and well he might do. For when the spring came less than a dozen of the two score men were still alive; and they looked like scarecrows.

Then, one bright morning when all the chill had gone from the air, and the buds were stirring on the apple-trees, Hereward came in with a thin rabbit in his hands and said, 'Morcar, we are well out of it, friend. William has fired the reeds, and the breeze is carrying the flames towards our old place. He will have a surprise!'

Morcar said, 'Put the rabbit in the pot, Hereward. Let us eat once again before we die.'

That afternoon the air was full of a great rumbling. They looked from their hidden shelter and saw wagon after wagon, drawn by weary horses, coming along the old causeway, high with timber. Beside them marched a whole army of men carrying saws and hammers and bags full of iron nails. Spearmen and archers followed them.

And that was how they first learned that the King meant to build a road across the fen from Aldreth to Ely, so that his soldiers could clear out the rebels once and for all time.

23. Escape

ON THE tenth day after the wagons had first come Hereward looked out from the old belfry of the ruin and said to his few friends, 'That road of William's is growing fast. It must be the better part of a mile long now. In another ten days he will have reached the mound, on the west side. Then he will march his men across it and will find—nothing but a dead sheep and a few plague corpses!'

He began to laugh so loudly then that a youth called Brant pulled him down out of sight and clapped a hand over his mouth.

'Have you gone mad, master?' said Brant. 'The workmen down there will hear you and what chance would we have?'

Hereward shook the lad off and nodded. 'Forgive me, friend,' he said. 'I am hungry and a bit weak in the head today. But the fit has passed. I shall not endanger you again.'

That night, when they were all asleep, Hereward made his way quietly from the old church, and set off towards Cambridge. He knew now what he must do; it had come to him suddenly, as though in a dream from God, and he saw no reason to doubt this dream.

Staggering, holding his rags together with a thin hand, he reached the north gate of the town, and, waiting in the shadows until the guard had turned, slipped inside, quiet as a cat.

There was a travellers' hostel that lay off the main street in a small alleyway beneath the wall, kept by a merry-faced old man who knew all that went on in the place. Hereward made for the door behind this house and knocked three times, very gently.

There was some shuffling behind the door, and then it was opened by a bent fellow who carried a horn lantern. Hereward had never seen the man before, and started to step back into the shadows. But the man with the lantern said softly, 'Why do you run away, lord? Are you afraid of a poor wretch like me, who have only enough strength to hold a lantern?'

Hereward said cautiously, 'Why do you call me lord?'

The man smiled, 'Because that is what you are—Lord Hereward. Do not look so amazed. All Cambridge knows what you look like—the King's heralds have proclaimed your appearance from the square every day for a month.'

Hereward said, 'That may be so. Who are you? There used to

be another landlord in this hostel. I have been here before in secret.'

The man with the lantern said, 'Alas, lord, I remember him well. Gilbert Vintner, they called him. The soldiers came at night and took him. I do not know what for—perhaps he was sheltering rogues and vagabonds. I do not know.'

He looked into Hereward's eyes for a moment, then said, 'It is well enough to shelter rogues and vagabonds, master—but in this trade it is just as important to be wise. Let us say that a rebel lord came to my house—then I would take him into my own chamber to dine and drink a cup of mulled ale; but I would never let him go into the room where the soldiers gather, or where some sharp-eyed prattler looking for a reward should see him.'

Hereward said, 'Is there a reward for me, host?'

The man shrugged his shoulders and said, 'Perhaps, master. Perhaps not. I pay little heed to such things. I gain my bread as honestly as I can. I am no Norman, lord.'

Hereward answered, 'And you are no Englishman, either. That tongue of yours would fit better round Flemish, I would guess.'

The host made a little bow and said, 'You have a quick ear, lord. But what matter? You English and we Flemish are cousins, are we not?'

He held the door open for Hereward to enter. For a moment Hereward hesitated, then, as he heard the mailed tramp of a soldier's footsteps at the corner, he decided that he would risk the hostel. The host held the lantern high so that he should not stumble on the ladder that went to an upper room. He followed after him and asked, 'What can I get for you, lord? A joint of venison that was sent up here for the King's own table? A flask of William's very wine? And both stolen from the wagon with no one the wiser! Would they suit you, with some fine white bread?'

Hereward sank on to a pile of straw that lay in a corner and said weakly, 'Aye, anything, as long as it is food. Good plain food. My stomach cries out for something other than acorns and grass.'

The man nodded and went away. He was soon back with a skin of red wine. Hereward drank deep before he could stop himself; it was so long since he had tasted anything like this. The wine ran down his throat, making him feel sleepy and merry at the same time. Then suddenly, all his hope, all his courage, came back. He smiled at the man and said, 'Look, friend, I did not come here simply to eat and drink while my comrades lay hungry in the fen. I came for a special reason. I must see the King, in person.'

The host nodded and smiled and scratched the end of his long nose. Then he said, 'Ah, you must see the King, hey? Is this not a strange thing, from you of all men?'

Hereward drank again from the skin and said, 'I want to make a bargain with him, you understand? I shall give myself up to him, so that he will let the others go free. They have lived like poor beasts for a year, and they have suffered enough.'

The man shook his head mournfully and said, 'Aye, poor lads, that they must have. And all for nothing—that's the saddest part of it all. All for nothing.'

Hereward bunched his fists to hear such words. Then he pulled himself together and said, 'You look a brisk fellow. Now can you, somehow, get word to the King that I am here? No, we will not say that I am here, until we know what his mind is. Let us say that I am *somewhere near*. That is right, somewhere near. . .'

The man nodded. 'Why, yes,' he said. 'We can do that, of a surety. Tell him that you are *somewhere near* and that you swear to deliver yourself to him, on the condition that Earl Morcar and young Brant, and a dozen others, go free. Is that it, master?'

Hereward gazed at the man sharply. Then he said, 'You seem to know who is with me, landlord. You even know how many fellows are left. How is that?'

The man said gently, 'In my trade, we learn a great deal, lord. Indeed, I have been waiting for you to knock on the back door every night since you left the barn. Every night since they laid the sheep and the dead men beside the mere to frighten you out of your fox-hole, lord.'

As he spoke he put the lantern down, and seemed to grow to twice his size in the flickering light. Hereward, dazed with the strong wine and exhausted with hunger, could hardly see the man. But what he did see was the dagger that had suddenly appeared in his right hand.

'Do not try to escape again, friend,' said the host. 'It has been trouble enough getting you into the trap—we cannot lose you now!'

Then Hereward saw that three mail-clad men stood in the shadow of the doorway, each bearing a bright sword.

One of them called out, 'So, is the wolf caught so easily? Good work, Gregoire! You made an excellent host! You would have tricked me as easily as you tricked this starving English fool.'

Then they came forward and began to rain blows on Hereward, one for each day he had kept them waiting, they said. It was not long before he lay still.

24. Dungeon

IN THE dark, it was hard to judge the passage of time. Hereward knew that he lay on straw and that his wrists and ankles were fastened with chains. But whether it was day or night he did not know, for there was no window in his cell. Sometimes, numbly, he heard the sound of bells; sometimes the clatter of horses' hooves.

And often, in the dark, he heard the scutter of small feet in the straw beside him.

A man came from time to time and left gruel in a wooden dish, which Hereward lapped up like a ravening dog.

The man would never speak to him, though Hereward begged for news.

'What day is it? How long have I been here? Will the King see me?'

To all these questions there was only silence, silence or a mocking laugh.

Hereward wondered at times whether this was death; or Hell; or Purgatory.

He tried to stand, but his leg-chains were bolted too closely into the stone wall, and so he fell. All he could do was to roll from side to side, at the limit of his short chain. And this, after a while, almost drove him mad; so he learned to lie still.

Then, at some time out of the endless blackness, the man said, 'You have been here a month, and there have been nothing but complaints from you. All night you moan and groan. How can I sleep when you do that?'

Hereward said, 'Tell me, am I blind? I cannot see you.'

The man laughed in the dark and said, 'You are not blind, as far as I know. But most of your fellows are, now. Young Brant is. They took one of his hands, too.'

Hereward clenched and unclenched his own hands. He had heard that men who lost a hand by a swift sword-cut in battle sometimes did not know it until much later. It seemed that he still had fingers and could move them. He was about to ask if he had lost a hand, too, when the man spoke again.

'You are a lucky devil,' he said. 'Luckier than the Earl Morcar. He's gone to Normandy with his feet chained to his neck. He'll rot in some dungeon where the sun has never shone since the world began. What do you think of that, fellow?'

Hereward did not answer, his brain was so bruised by the man's words. He did not even know whether a man had spoken, or whether in the dark he had dreamed the words.

Then the man kicked him in the ribs, and Hereward knew that it was no dream.

The man said, 'You are lucky, are you not, Hereward? Better men than you lie dead or blind. Say you are lucky. Say it so that I can hear it. Then I will leave you.'

But Hereward would not speak now, and the man kicked him a few times, then left him.

Part Four

1072 - 1077

25. Queen Matilda

THEN ONE day the low door to the dungeon, which was in an old wine-cellar below the tavern, was kicked open, and three men entered carrying lights. One was the gaoler; the other two were mail-clad soldiers who carried daggers in their hands. Hereward, lying on the mouldering straw, his wrists and ankles chafed by his rusty chains, turned weakly from the light of their torches and shut his eyes.

The gaoler said, 'They get like this, even the bravest of them, after a few months in the dark on short commons.'

He began to laugh loudly, but one of the soldiers said, 'Silence, fat-belly. This is a warrior, a brave one—something you will never be. Strike off the chains and count yourself lucky that you are not lying on the straw in his place.'

The gaoler complained, saying that it was always the same with soldiers—they thought they owned the world and that common men were their slaves.

The other soldier laughed menacingly and said, 'Well, is that not right and proper, man? Knock off the chains and keep your grumbling for your old woman when you sit over the fire with her. She may listen to you, but we shall not.'

It was a painful affair, getting the chains off. It was even more painful for Hereward to stand upright again. His limbs hardly seemed to belong to him, and he felt so dazed that he almost fell to the stone floor. The soldiers supported him and led him up to a chamber where they washed him and combed his straggling hair, and even put a fresh tunic on his thin body. When one of them poured wine between his lips, Hereward said at last, 'Why do you do this, butchers? Cannot you leave a man to die quietly in the dark?'

The taller of the soldiers said shortly, 'Thegn, we obey the orders of our King—no more and no less. There may be time enough for you to die in the dark after he has spoken to you. Until then, drink this wine and try to bear yourself like a man. You will be carried through the streets of Cambridge in a closed litter to the place where William waits for you.'

Hereward gazed at the big sword which the soldier wore. The man noticed this and said with a laugh, 'Do not be a fool, Thegn Hereward; you are too weak to swing such a weapon. And even if you could, the passage-ways and gates are thronged with good honest Normans. You would never get away, through to the streets.'

Hereward said, 'That is a foolish use of words—*good, honest Normans*. There are none of those living.'

The soldier nodded. 'I should say the same, no doubt,' he answered, 'if I sat where you do today, and you were the one with the helmet and the long sword. Come, let us be away. We must not keep the King waiting.'

In the litter, with its closed hide curtains, Hereward was almost sick. He had not eaten for so long, and the strong resinous wine, together with the swaying motion of the litter, made his head reel. But at last he was set down and then hurried across a narrow street and up stone stairs to a long dark chamber, where the shutters were closed, and only a few tapers shed a dim light. Hereward could see that in various parts of the room mail-clad knights stood, talking to each other in low voices. They hardly seemed to notice his entrance. Among them was a tall, broad-shouldered man who wore the robes of a bishop over his mail, and carried a leaden mace carelessly in his hand, with which he emphasized his words. No one needed to say that this was the king's half-brother, Odo of Bayeux. There was no other man like him in England—strong both in Church and in State, the regent of the King himself.

Odo was laughing at some jest when the tapestries at the far end of the chamber parted and King William came in. At either side of him walked a man. The lord at the King's right hand was smiling and demonstrating some point with his fine, gold-ringed hands.

One of the soldiers said, 'Waltheof seems content today!' Hereward saw that Waltheof's hair was cropped short, and no longer flowed freely to his shoulders as he had once worn it, when he was the hero of the English at the time of the York rebellion.

The man on the King's other side was young and dark-haired. He had a sulky pale face and pulled at his lower lip as though dissatisfied about something. From the lions embroidered on his tunic, Hereward guessed that this was Robert, Robert Curthose, William's eldest son, who would one day become Duke of Normandy.

As the King came down the room and sat in the tall oak chair at its centre the knights and barons kneeled. Only Hereward still stood. Someone whispered, 'Down, Englishman! Down before your King.'

But Hereward did not reply or move. And at last the King waved his hand sternly and the many men filed out through the tall door, leaving only Robert and Earl Waltheof behind. Bishop Odo went with a bad grace, muttering loudly, and even striking with his leaden mace against the wooden shutters.

King William smiled at this, but said nothing.

At last he looked at Hereward and said in a low but firm voice, 'Come nearer, thegn. I am a little too weary to shout the length of the room. It is a long time since we fished together on Axholme.'

He was dressed in an ordinary leather jerkin and linen trousers, cross-banded to the ankle in the English manner. Over his shoulders he wore a cloak of red serge, and on his head a light iron helmet without ear-guards or nose-piece. Apart from his great ring and the broad leather belt round which careered the lions of Normandy, cast in silver, there was nothing to indicate that this was the Conqueror of the English.

Hereward stood before him a while, then said, 'What do you want with me? I have no wish to talk of fishing—or Axholme or anything else. I shall tell you nothing. I am content to be beheaded like a hundred more, or to be cast into your dungeons for life, like Morcar, or that brother of Harold Godwinson, Wulfnoth. Wulfnoth did you no wrong, Norman. He was the only one of his brood of whom this can be said—but it is true. Very well, kill me or put me where Wulfnoth is. I do not care.'

The King was silent for a while, then he said slowly, 'It seems you are determined to ruin God's handiwork, thegn.'

Hereward flared up at this and said, 'Dare you speak of ruin, when half England still lies smouldering? When the folk of the north crawl starving on their bellies like dogs, seeking the scraps of offal that even your hunting-hounds refuse?'

Robert of Normandy stopped pulling at his lip, and began to grin at these words. But Earl Waltheof held up his hand towards Hereward and said urgently, 'Thegn, this is not the time for hot words. Learn discretion, my friend.'

Hereward looked at him, speechless, to think that this lord who had led the English in the rising at York should have changed so.

Then William spoke again, this time gravely and in an even voice, and said, 'You speak out as your heart dictates, thegn. You are honest, though misguided. Perhaps, if you were a king you would think differently. You must thank God that you are not a king; for a king must often do what makes him weep afterwards in the loneliness of his bed.'

Hereward ground his teeth and said, 'You talk like a coward, not a king.'

William drew a deep breath and then replied, 'That is perhaps because I am a coward. I have been in too many affrays not to feel the chill sweat of fear. It is only the monks in their safe cells who are not cowards. They can set down brave deeds in their books without feeling anything but reflected glory. Though, no doubt, some of them came near to feeling fear the day you sacked the Golden Borough, my Christian friend.'

Hereward clenched his fists as though he wished to strike the King down. But William pointed a finger at him and said, 'Do nothing rash, thegn. I only tell you that, in the eyes of many men, you are as much a destroyer, a burner of villages, a robber of churches, as I am. We each have our reasons—but could either of us persuade the peasants that we meant well?'

At last Hereward said in a tight voice, 'Do not play with me any longer, Tanner. I am not a hide to be beaten and then softened in the brine-tub. Punish me and be finished.'

For a moment William's face hardened. It had been many years since anyone had used this old insult against him; many years since a man dared to remind him that his mother, Arlette, had been the daughter of a tanner. . . . It was at Alençon—and thirty-two men had lost their hands and feet for crying, 'Tanner! Tanner!' over the city walls at him.

But that was half a lifetime ago. A man learns to tolerate many things in such a space. Especially a man like William, who had at last gained his heart's desire, his kingdom.

Almost gently, he said to Hereward, 'The least said, the soonest mended, my friend. I will come to the point—I think that you have been punished enough, one way and another. I am not one to punish twice over for the same misdeed. Ask Earl Waltheof if that is not true. So, this is what I say to you: you have shown me that you are a man skilled in war; you have shown that you are a man respected by your own folk. The English would obey a war-leader like you, and in obeying you they would save their own lives—if you, in your turn, obeyed me. Earl Waltheof once thought otherwise—but now he has made himself my friend, and so the friend of his countrymen. Is that not so, Earl?'

Waltheof nodded and bowed his head. Hereward bit his lips and was silent.

William went on, 'In this world, thegn, there is nothing perfect. My brother, Odo, could prove that to you at great length, and with quotations from Greek, Hebrew, and Latin to make his point. I am no scholar, so you must take my word for it without quotations. And I tell you that on earth, though a man may dream of drinking from a silver chalice, he must often be content with a clay cup. So you must be content with me—though you may have dreamed that some other man, Hardrada of Norway, or the Atheling, perhaps, should have been your king.'

Hereward said in a shaking voice, 'You know that I hate you, yet you seem to be offering me my freedom. Is that so?'

The King kicked at a smouldering log in the hearth as though

131

to give himself time to think, then, with narrowed eyes, looked at Hereward and nodded.

'I am offering you not only your freedom, but also a baron's state. Do not set too much store by that, it would only be a small tenancy—somewhere in Lincolnshire. Perhaps the lands your father once held. As a baron, a lesser baron, you would hold lands from me, and you would learn to see sense. You would learn to accept the world as it is—and not as you dreamed it to be. What do you say?'

Hereward's blood began to pulse so fast now that he almost sank to his knees. There was both relief and anger mixed in his brain; and he did not know what to say.

William said, 'Sit down, thegn. You are weary. You have fought a long fight and have suffered the necessary punishment. I am a soldier and I speak plainly. Sit down.'

Hereward felt the King leading him to a stool beside the fire. He wanted to drag away, to strike at the man, but he lacked the strength. He knew that tears were running down his stubbled cheeks and into his beard, but he could not stop them. He put his hands over his face.

At last he said, 'If only I had my wife and son again, you could keep your barony. You could swelter in Hell for all I cared about you, or about England! That is my answer.'

There was a long silence in the chamber after Hereward had said these words; a silence so deep that for a time he thought he was dreaming it all in the dungeon where he had lain so long.

Then the King said in a firm voice, 'And this is my answer!'

And the quietness seemed to lift as though the shutters of the room had been flung open to let in the sunlit air. Hereward felt a gentle touch on his shoulder.

He slowly raised his head and saw Euphemia. She was standing before him, smiling sadly, and dressed in blue and white. Beside her, holding her hand, stood a boy about nine years old, his wide grey eyes fixed curiously on Hereward, his mouth half-laughing and half-crying. On his right arm the boy wore a bronze bracelet embossed with boars and hounds. This had once been the property of Hardrada, and had been left as a birth-gift at Bergen years ago, before the longships had set course for the Humber.

Euphemia said, 'This is Cnut, your son, Hereward. He has grown to be a fine boy. A warrior could be pleased with such a son.' Then she seemed to wait for an answer.

But Hereward could not speak. He rose unsteadily and put an arm about each of them, drawing them towards him and hugging them silently.

Looking beyond them, his eyes now dim, Hereward saw that the King was smiling strangely; but smiling; as though thinking that every man, however brave or rebellious, had his price—and that often this price was the simplest of gifts.

But Hereward was too occupied now to think of such things, or of vengeances and glory. His wife and his son were with him after years of waiting and he was glad, living for once only in the present.

All at once Cnut pulled himself free and got to his knees at his father's feet. As Hereward smiled down at him, the boy took hold of his hands and said in a clear voice, 'Ic becom eowr man.' This was the act of homage of a thegn to his lord, as old as the Saxon folk themselves: 'I am your man.'

Hereward turned to his wife and said, 'He has been taught well, Euphemia. I spoke those words to Hardrada, years ago, in the hall at Bergen and he understood me. Who taught him this?'

Euphemia did not reply. The answer was given by another woman, who had come quietly into the dim chamber and now stood beside the King, pale-faced and smiling, her delicate white hands clasped over the golden cross which glinted on the wine-dark red of her robe.

This woman said, 'I taught your son, Baron. I, sister of Flemish Baldwin and wife of the King, taught him. It is proper that the son of an Englishman should speak his oath of fealty in his own tongue.'

Hereward bowed his head now before Queen Matilda, the daughter of one Baldwin and the sister of another. Nor did he think that this was any dishonour, for her reputation was great

133

in the countries of the north, both as a pious queen and as a stern one. This was the Flemish queen who had ruled Normandy for William while he was gaining the throne at Hastings, and who had kept rebel barons in check during the burning of the north. The patron of scholars, the almsgiver to the poor, the worshipper of Christ; Matilda was all these things. And now Hereward knelt before her, unable to help himself.

'Lady,' he said, 'tell me that it is you who give me back my family. Then I am your servant. I will bow the knee to you, lady.'

Queen Matilda shook her head a little sadly and said, 'It is God who gives, not I. And it is God who instructs you, through your son. Speak to the anointed King those same words which your son has just spoken to you, Baron. So all will be well.'

Then she stepped back into the shadows.

For a while, Hereward glared at King William, his old pride battling with his love for Euphemia and Cnut.

Then, awkwardly, he said, 'Do you hope to gain my loyalty in this way, Norman?'

King William was long in answering. At last, he said, 'When I bought your wife and son from Swein of Denmark, I thought it was a good bargain if, by using them, I could bring you peacefully over to my side. Now, for some strange reason, I am not certain that I acted well. For, as my own wife has reminded me, it is your right, under God's law, to live with your own folk. It is not a privilege that should be granted by an earthly king.'

He paused for an instant and looked away. Then, in a firm voice, he went on, 'Take your wife and son, thegn, and leave this house without delay. There will be horses for you. Go where you choose, and go now, before I change my mind.'

Hereward heard these words, bewildered. No one in his life-time had spoken to him so fairly—unless it had been Hardrada.

Unable to help himself, he suddenly took William's hands in his own and, kneeling, said, 'Ic becom eowr man.'

Hereward heard his own words as though they had been spoken by a stranger. He felt the King's hands shaking strangely as he answered.

'In the presence of these witnesses, I, William of England and Duke of Normandy, accept your oath, Hereward. And in that same presence I here create you baron. By God's grace, let there be peace between us always.'

26. Baron

IN THIS way Hereward became a baron and accepted King William as his lord. His lands were not great, but they stretched between Peterborough and Grantham, into Kesteven, the southern Riding of Lincolnshire.

He wanted no castle, for, as he told his overlord Bishop Odo, he had seen enough of war and now wished only to farm as his father had once done, and to watch his son grow up in the sun.

Bishop Odo laughed at this and said, 'We'll see, Baron—we'll see! But at least you must follow our custom and keep armed knights on your holding, in case the King needs them. Ten will be enough—good strong youths who can sit a horse and use a lance. They can be Englishmen, if you wish, as long as they take the oath to the King, to me and to you. That will bind them tight enough. And, in return, you must allow them small-holdings, so that they can live well without turning brigand and robbing travellers along the highway.'

This Hereward agreed to; but his own mind was set on the

house he would build for his wife and son. When it was finished it stood on a hillock above the river and looked down on the oak forest that billowed towards Stamford. It was a house of oak and plaster, with some of its roofs thatched, and some covered with bright red tiles fetched from the Humberside. All who saw the house, Baron's Steading, said how much it brought back memories of the old Danelaw. Its main roof soared high and steep, and was surmounted by a dragon carved in black oak. All the facing-timbers were carved so intricately that they looked more like lace than wood. 'Aye,' answered Hereward, 'there is still something we men of the north can show the Normans, when it comes to building a house.'

William came to Baron's Steading sometimes. And once he made Hereward a surprise gift of honey-coloured stone brought from Caen in Normandy.

'This will build you a winter room,' he said. 'And every evening when you sit in it, you will remind yourself of me, my friend.'

But Hereward did not use the stone for a room. Instead, he had made a small chapel, much after the Byzantine style, behind the steading at a quiet place where the oak woods came down to the stockade. This gave delight to Euphemia, who never wearied of giving thanks to God for the return of her husband.

Once when the King came in through the gates, after hunting up along Market Rasen with his half-brother one bleak November day, Hereward was out in the yard chopping wood for the fire, taking turn and turn about with the thralls of the household.

He stood in his thick leather jacket, wiping the sweat from his forehead as William rode in, like a ship floating on a sea of hounds.

The King called out, red-faced with the harsh wind, 'Good day, Baron. I didn't expect to find you playing the kitchen-man! Come, is there not a cup of ale for the King?'

While Bishop Odo sat with young Cnut, showing him a new move in the game of chess, William lounged with his jerkin off near the roaring fire, praising Euphemia's spiced beer and honey-cakes.

'You must show the Queen how this is done,' he said, his

136

mouth stuffed full. 'We Normans pay more heed to our castles than our tables. With you English it is the other way.'

Then he looked round and shrugged his shoulders. 'Yet, seeing the comforts of this house, I begin to wonder. . . . You have carpets on your floor. How is that?'

Euphemia said, 'We always had carpets in my father's house in Miklagard. I do not care for rushes; they smell so much after they have been down a while. So a trader brought these into Boston port for the Baron.'

William looked shrewdly at Hereward, then said, 'You are becoming a good man about the house, Baron, hey?'

Hereward smiled and said, 'Once I lived so long among reeds and rushes that I never want to see them again, lord.'

William nodded. 'I hated Ely as much as you, Baron. But it was God's will—and it brought us together after all. These things have their purposes, if only a man can live long enough to see that purpose.'

Suddenly Bishop Odo gave a great shout and slapped the oaken table with his fist. 'This lad of yours has got my king in check, Hereward!' he said. 'He learns a mite too fast for my old brains! Let me have him with me at my castle for a while, and we'll make a masterly captain of him. A man who can move his pieces cleverly can move men the same way. Let me have him, can I?'

Euphemia bit her lip, but said, 'If it is your wish, my lord Bishop. But only for a little while, I beg you.'

King William frowned a while, then said, 'My brother's request makes mine the more difficult.'

Hereward, who had looked forward to having Cnut with him for the hunting that winter, said suspiciously, 'What is your request, my lord?'

William poured himself another cup of beer, then answered, 'My wife, the Queen, is greatly taken with your lady, Euphemia, Baron. Indeed, I am here today at her wish—to beg you to spare your wife for a month or two, so that she may travel into Normandy with the Queen.'

Hereward began to pace the room in doubt. At last he said,

'I mean no disrespect, my lord, but has the Queen no other lady to go with her?'

William started to play with his cup. 'You talk like a young lover who cannot bear to be parted from his sweetheart,' he said, 'instead of a gnarled old warrior with a heart of flint! Well, I will come to the point, Baron; the Queen is engaged on a great work— a piece of embroidery, of stitchery of some sort, and she wants your wife to help her. There will be a score of others at it, all stitching away—but the Queen feels that they should follow a different mode from the one they learn in Normandy. Matilda has a passion to set down things in the Byzantine manner. You know what an attraction the East has for us Normans, these days? So many of our people go out there, to gain a kingdom.'

Hereward asked, puzzled, 'Set down what things, lord?'

Bishop Odo began to cough, as though his drink had gone down the wrong way. But the King answered without hesitation, 'To tell the truth, Baron, the Queen has turned historian, and wishes to show the story of Normandy in a great tapestry.'

Hereward stood by the King's chair and said, 'To tell how Harold lied in his oath over the holy bones; and how you came with horses in ships and a wooden castle, to draw him down from Stamfordbridge and punish him with death. That is what you want to tell, King?'

The King's dark face grew suddenly grim and his smile was not that of a man who makes a joke. He nodded, then waited for Hereward to reply.

Hereward walked through the stillness of the room to the window, and there he saw a wasp buzzing angrily. He looked down at it, as it ran here and there on the stone ledge, then slowly crushed it with his horny thumbnail. He watched it, struggling in two pieces, for a while. Then he turned and said, 'Very well, lord. Let us get into the new year, with the blossom on the boughs, and then you shall take my wife with you to Normandy to stitch with the Queen. And you, Bishop, shall borrow my son for a space. So, it is agreed.'

The King came up to him and said, 'Let's have no bad blood

about this, Baron. Every great lady serves her queen at some time, and every youth goes to another lord to learn the use of arms and how to carve a joint of beef. There's nothing strange about it.'

For a while Hereward gazed at the carpet-covered floor. Then he looked William in the eye and said, 'Only this, that I am not like the rest of your tenants, King. I have seen little of my wife or my son since God gave them to me. Now it seems I am to see even less of them.'

Bishop Odo swaggered from the table, his cup in his hand, and said merrily, 'Still playing the old fox, Hereward? Still asking for a better bargain? Well, doubtless it can be arranged. Most of the tenants-in-chief hold other appointments at the court; butlers, chamberlains, stewards. Even men like Robert Malet and William fitz Osbern. So why not you? How would it suit you to be King's Steward, somewhere or other? With a place at the King's board, and a good picking off the land?'

Hereward raised his right hand on an impulse, as though he would strike the Bishop. Odo did not move, but his red face became fixed in its smile and something of a warning flashed out from his light grey eyes.

The King hit at the table-top with the flat of his hand. 'Splendeur de Dieu!' he shouted. 'Would you strike a bishop? A royal prince? What sort of man are you, Baron? You'd cut off your nose to spite your face, it seems.'

Hereward turned away and said quietly, 'I ask your pardon, both of you. I am overwrought. It is the cold in my bones, perhaps. I can hardly bend my right leg to find the stirrup some days now. I must be getting old.'

The King clapped him on the shoulder and said, 'We'll cure that, Baron. All you need is more hunting. We will ride after the tall deer, friend. That will do the trick. And, meantime, think well of what Odo said. It is no dishonour to be King's Steward. In great Alfred's day, there were the horse-thegns, who served their king; and in Cnut's time, there were the stallers, the "place men". And I have yet to hear that they felt demeaned by setting the king's dishes before him at table. Think about it, Baron.'

When the two men had gone Hereward went back to the window ledge and watched the dead wasp's nerves still twitching the legs and the pincers.

His wife and son waited long for him to turn and talk to them; then at last they left the room and went to Euphemia's bower together, unable to bear his sadness.

27. A Man Alone

SPRING CAME and went; and with it went Hereward's wife and his son. Hereward hardly said a word of farewell to them, he was so locked up in his own grief. Euphemia travelled from the house in a covered litter, her face veiled, her lips tight and her hands trembling. Before the men lifted the litter, she leaned out and said, 'Baron, my dear one, it will not be long. I shall be with you again before the year is out. I shall count the days as carefully as you do, I promise you.'

Robert Curthose, the Prince, himself came to fetch young Cnut, riding a big bay gelding and laughing loud about the hall. Cnut was glad to go with the young prince, trotting beside him on the dappled grey that Hereward had given him—so that he could hunt with his father through the Lincoln woods. Now he was riding that horse away, but at twelve he was too young to think of this.

When they had gone Hereward walked like an old man into the buttery and took down a cobwebbed ale-flask from a shelf. Then he sat on the cold stone that the cooks used to keep the milk fresh. He did not budge until he had finished the ale. And when he tried to stand his legs failed him. The servants found him the next day, snoring on the buttery floor, the flask empty, and his tunic spattered with its dregs.

When they got him to his bed his limbs were shaking with an ague after the night in the cold. A Jewish leech rode all the way from Lincoln to tend him. He said to Hereward, 'My lord, you are no longer a youth. Young men can lie out all night under trees or hedges, hunting, and come to no harm. But a man of fifty-four should take more care, should think more of a fur-lined gown and a snug place beside the chimney.'

These words so stung Hereward that he struck out at the kindly leech and began to shout the worst abuse he could think of.

One of the house-knights paid the leech off and sent him back to Lincoln. And when the knight went up to his lord's room he found Hereward struggling to lace on his heavy leather jerkin and staggering about the place as though he had lost his sense of balance.

'Baron,' said the knight, 'what are you thinking of? You should be in bed.'

Hereward crawled to the oak chest where his sword lay and tried to drag the weapon from its wrappings. The knight knew then that there would be little profit in trying to reason with his lord. He went down the stairs and told the butler what had happened, and after that few would dare go up to him, except a young girl named Asa, whose folk were northerners from Wark. She was a bought-woman, a slave, whose widowed mother had sold her after the burning of the north so as to feed her little brothers and sisters. She was very thin and quite simple. Most of the time she hardly understood what was said to her, in English or French, for her own family language had been a sort of Danish that the men of Wark still spoke.

Asa went to Hereward and took him beef-broth and bread, and a stone jar of barley beer. At first he hit out at the food and sent it skimming; but she picked it up patiently and handed it to him again. Then, in Danish, she said, 'Eat this, master, and be well again.'

The great fighter gazed at her in bewilderment. She was so thin, and her face so pale. He sat on the bed and drew her to him, stroking her straw-coloured hair.

Then he said in Danish, 'Thou art a tiny mite to be out-facing such as me.'

Asa said, 'I'm not feared o' you, master. My dad was a man like you. And maybe even a harder hitter, master. I'm used to that. All I want is for you to get well, master. Then we'll have some law and order in this house again.'

Hereward made her sit beside him. Then when he had shared the food and drink with her, he said, 'What is happening in this house, then, lass?'

Asa said, 'The stewards are selling meal and meat and the sawyers have given up work at the barns. We've lost thirty head of cattle since you took to your room, master. And the knights swear they'll ride off and serve another lord who is better worth their swords.'

Hereward stared at her with bleared eyes for a while, then said, 'How long have I been sick?'

Asa counted on her fingers and answered, 'Nigh on a month, master. And come another month there'll be nobbut a few sticks and stones left here. And the servants all gone.'

Hereward said, 'Then we'll quicken them up a bit.'

So he put on his iron byrnie and got out his long sword, and went down into the house. It was hard going, for he was a heavy man and the hand-rails were flimsy ones. He fell three times before he reached the hall. The knights and serving-folk clustered in the doorway, wondering what to do. Hereward sent them all packing and followed them out of the gate, shaking his sword at them. The

142

knights shrugged their shoulders and pretended not to care, but they saw to it that they were out of striking distance all the same.

And then Hereward called Asa down and said to her, 'It seems I lost a wife and a son—and found a little daughter.'

Asa shook her head and said, 'Nay, master, I'm no man's daughter. But I'll be thy kitchen-wench, and I'll wash thy shirts and comb thy hair when it gets lugs in it.'

The next day Hereward took iron nails and closed the stockade gate so that no one could enter. Then he had a table and stools and bedding moved into a shed that his carpenters once used, and there he set up his home with Asa.

'This'll be less work for you, lass,' he said. 'And less wood-chopping for me to keep us warm, hey?'

Asa said, 'This is like the house I used to live in at Wark, with my brothers and sisters in the good days. I have no liking for great barn-like places, like your hall. I get nightmares in yon places, and think the trolls be a-coming for me at night-time. But here all's snug, master!'

Hereward laughed for the first time for weeks, and told Asa some old tales he remembered about Beowulf and Grettir, brave warriors who lay in halls at midnight and caught the trolls and ghosts when they came looking for their prey among the sleepers.

Asa grew to like Hereward; but in his heart he was still unhappy. And at night he tossed and turned and had dreams of loneliness and death.

Then one day there was a great shouting outside the stockade and a messenger cried out, 'Baron, open the gate. I have a letter, for you.'

Hereward called back, 'Throw it over the wall and be off with you. There's no wine for you in this house. That day is past.'

The youth grumbled, but he flung the letter over and rode away.

Hereward sat on a pile of wood to read it as best he could. It was from his son, Cnut, and written by a scribe in a stilted manner.

It said: 'Honoured sir, the Prince reminds me of my duty to write to you, or else I should have forgotten it. My horse, the one you gave me, is of little use in the rough countryside of Normandy. The Prince has given me another, a better one. He is brave and generous, and the man I most love. One day, when he is a great king, I shall serve him wherever he commands me. He speaks of going to the Holy Land one day. I pray to God that this may be so. I shall ride with him, God willing. I have seen my mother briefly. She is well, at the work the Queen has set her to. Our family is honoured by this task, noble father. Last night I dreamed of you riding and laughing among the trees, the merriest man on earth. I woke envious to think that you should be so well pleased with life. The priest here says that the dream was a good omen, and that you must be merry indeed for the news to come by night all the way from England to Normandy. God be with my merry father, in all courtesy, Cnut.'

For a while after he had read these words Hereward could hardly see. But at last he wiped his eyes, then went into the house and sat in a dark corner. Later he tried to tear the letter up, but the parchment was too strong for him, so he flung it on to the fire as it was, and watched the sheepskin smoulder.

Asa came to him and said, "'Twas bad news, master, then?'

Hereward nodded and said, 'Aye, bad news. I have lost my son again, I think.'

He said no more about it, and that night went early to bed and told no more stories. He said that the day had tired him. But Asa heard him muttering all night in his sleep, and sometimes laughing out in a cold and bitter way.

A few weeks after this the King came. There was no warning of his coming. Only a blast on the horn as his troop of riders came over the hill and the loud drumming of the horses' hooves.

Hereward was sitting outside the stockade, scraping hides with some fellows from the village, his own serfs. He had wagered them that he could prepare four hides to their one, and seemed to be winning, until the King's men came.

William was leading them, dressed plainly in grey hunting clothes and wearing a woollen cap on his head.

He sat looking at Hereward for a while, then said, 'I didn't think to find the Baron scraping greasy hides when I came to visit him.'

Hereward spat in the fire and said, 'I could be at worse trades, King.'

The King smiled and said, 'Yes, and you could be at better, Baron. Send these louts about their business, and get yourself ready for hunting with me today. While you do that I will sit by your fire and drink some of your good beer.'

Hereward said slowly, 'There's no fire, and no beer. And if you want me out hunting, then I must come as I am, for my gear is locked up in a chest and the key is mislaid.'

Two of the knights drove the serfs away, while the King dismounted and took Hereward aside. 'Friend,' he said firmly, 'there is much in you that I like; but there is also much that needs correction. A baron is not an ordinary man, Hereward. A baron must pay heed to his state, and must . . .'

But Hereward would not let the King finish. He broke in and said, 'Must, must, must! Is that the only word you Normans can say? As for my not being an ordinary man, I'll give that the lie straightway. Let me tell you that my father was a small thegn—a farmer, William. Just as your mother was a tanner's daughter. So how noble does that make us?'

The King gazed at Hereward as though he would have struck him down. His face was as dark as a thunder-cloud, and his eyes seemed to be straining from their sockets.

Hereward laughed in the King's face and went on, 'As for correcting me, first correct your own son, Robert Curthose, for stealing my son from me. But I warn you, don't come here to correct me, or you will find a man that does not take kindly to the whip.'

As he spoke Hereward stressed his words with the scraping-knife that he still held in his right hand.

A knight who rode behind the King took this as a threat to the King and pushed his horse forward until it pressed Hereward against the wall of his house.

But William called out to the knight to draw away. Then he went to Hereward and said quietly, so that no one else should hear,

'For God's sake, Hereward, let us behave like grown men, not like boys or old berserks. We are neither, at our age. Come with me riding, and let us put our differences to rights.'

Hereward threw the scraping-knife into the grass and nodded in a surly way. Then he turned and went the back way to his stables. The King and the knights sat outside all the time he was away, without food or drink. And when Hereward appeared again he was sitting on the sorriest nag he could find. Even his harness was pieced together with twine. It was as though he was trying his hardest to offend the King.

And so they went hunting that day into the Kesteven marshes, and up towards Grantham.

One of the barons who rode behind them said to another, 'This Englishman is not likely to keep his head on his shoulders for long, if you ask me. He has pressed the King to the furthest limit, I would guess.'

28. The Quarrel

BUT THE baron had guessed wrong. Before the day was out Hereward had gone further. It was as though a devil had got into him, and was driving him on to destruction.

After they had been riding half the afternoon, they started a tall buck with antlers like trees sprouting from his head. Because of the soft ground, the creature was soon blown and stood at bay, trembling and bewildered by the shouting men and plunging horses. It was the only deer they had seen that day, and the knights drew back so that the King should be first in at the kill, as was his right.

Yet, just as William set his horse at the run and had his short spear levelled, Hereward came in suddenly from the side and flung his own spear, which rattled on the tines of the buck's antlers to wake the beast from his trance and send him galloping into a narrow tree-hung gully where he could not be followed.

William reined in his horse, then swung round furiously on Hereward.

'Splendeur de Dieu!' he began; but Hereward laughed in his face and bent to pick up his spear.

Then he called to one of the knights, 'That was a shrewd cast—to strike without harming. It is a trick I must practise more often. It looks well!'

No one spoke, for the King's face was like thunder.

'How far do you think you can travel along this road, Baron?' he asked. 'Did you not see that this was my quarry?'

Hereward began to pick his teeth contemptuously with the point of a skinning-knife. Then he said, 'I heard you cry out "Haro!" '

William looked at him, bewildered.

'That I did,' he said. 'And I have a right to. It is my call.'

Hereward said, putting on a silly smile, 'I forgot that. I heard the word "Haro!" and it put me in mind of Harold, Godwine's son. So I flung my spear at Harold, not at the buck. As for the buck, you can have him and welcome, if you are as hungry as that, King of England. All you have to do is find him again.'

Then he remounted his shuddering nag and turned his back on the King.

William sat hunched in the saddle, his white-knuckled hands gripping the high pommel, like a man about to have a fit. One of the barons came up to him and whispered, 'Say the word, sir, and I will see that this jack-ape troubles you no more.'

King William shuddered, then shook his head. 'I will do my own work, Gil,' he said, 'when it needs to be done. And that is not yet. Leave me now.'

They rode until they got clear of the trees; the King in front, his heavy cloak wrapped round his ears, speaking to no one. Hereward cantered well to the side, at times singing an old Norwegian rowing-song, and at other times drinking from a beerhorn which was slung from his saddle. He seemed to ride in another world; and so did the King. But their worlds were not the same ones.

By sunset they reached a manor that lay in the fief of Robert Mortain, on a small island of solid ground to the south of Grantham. Here the royal party was to spend the night, and a steward came out of the gate with cups of mulled wine to offer the horsemen.

Hereward pushed past him, ignoring the offer, and leaving the King and the knights to drink alone. He was first through the gate, and soon they all heard his voice shouting out that they had come to a barbarous pigsty.

The King went forward, his face white, to see Hereward waving his arms and letting his horse rear where it wished, knocking over trestles and barrels.

The reason for his anger was soon seen. A half-starved fellow, dressed in rags, was hanging from a rough gallows, his hands tied behind his back. Below him lay another, tended by two monks. His head and chest had been wounded, and the monks were hard put to it to staunch the blood. On the dusty ground lay two horn-picks, shaped much like battle-axes.

Hereward was shouting, 'You Norman swine! To set plough-men on to each other in combat! Is this your justice?'

He bent from the saddle and tore a wooden support from the gallows. Then, with a great heave, he flung the baulk of wood through a window of the manor, breaking the carved shutters.

The King came up to him and said through clenched teeth, 'For the love of God, Baron! You break our law. It is the old law for men who have a difference to fight it out with the horn-picks. It is the ordeal by combat, and neither you nor I can change it.'

Hereward turned red eyes upon the King and said for all to hear, 'Your great Norman law—to let scullions and farriers use *weapons* on each other, as though they were knights? Is it justice to turn a blacksmith on to a pot-boy? Next you will be setting monks to fight apple-women, you Normans.'

While the King raged, Hereward drew his knife and sawed at

148

the rope from which the dead peasant swung. Then, with the body over his saddle-bow, he cantered round the courtyard calling out to the peasants who had assembled near the walls, 'Whose son is this? Whose father is this? Whose brother is this? Take him and give him decent burial. Hereward will pay the church dues.'

A group of ragged men and women came forward and took the body, weeping.

One old woman, with a black shawl about her white head, said, 'I wish to God you had got here an hour before, Baron. Then my son would still be alive. I wish to God that there were more like you in this land.'

Hereward gazed down at her and said, 'I am as English as you are. When I have gone, some of these Norman pigs may wish to root you out of your hovel. Some of them may wish to show what brave fellows they are by whipping an old woman whose son they have let be murdered. But if they do, mother, if they raise as much as one finger against you, I swear now upon Holy Cross that I shall hear about it, and I shall come again. And I swear then that Robert Mortain must build himself another house, for I shall not leave one stone standing on another here. And Mortain must get himself another crew of ruffians to guard him, for there shall be gallows set about this courtyard from which his minions shall swing like bunches of grapes.'

The peasants became excited then, and one of them even ran towards the King's horse as though he meant to take the bridle. Shocked, one of the knights set his horse forward at the shag-haired fellow, but the King halted him and said, 'Let it be. This is not the time to meddle, Alain.'

Then he turned his horse away from the peasant and the hunting-party went into the house where the trembling steward waited to greet them.

Hereward did not go in with them, but rode up the steps to the hall and shouted after them, 'A mad baron to match a mad king! And soon, William, there will be scores of mad barons—and still only one mad king to keep them in check. Then the fires will start to burn!'

He swung about and rode from the courtyard, with the peasants crying after him.

King William sat shaking with rage in the hall, his hands as powerless as though he suffered from palsy. No one dared come near to him.

It was old Gil who knelt by him at last and offered him a wine-cup. 'What is to be done, sir?' he asked.

William began to sip the wine, spilling much of it down the breast of his tunic. He answered with the shambling, halting speech of one who has been badly hurt.

'Nothing yet, Gil. But soon, by God's Resurrection and Splendour, I must put a curb on this mad old stallion. There is no other way.'

29. The King's Letter

IT WAS the best part of a week before Hereward got back to his house. He spent his time among the villages, drinking and fighting with any peasant who would take him on. He always won, whether at wrestling or quarter-staff; but no man bore him ill will on account of this.

So he worked off his great anger against the King. But anger was replaced by sadness, for when he reached the house once more and called out for Asa he found that the girl had gone.

One of his serfs told him that she had been afraid to stay in the house alone, and thought he had left for ever. So she had packed up her few small belongings and had set off on foot for the north—to see if she could find her own folk, she had said.

For a month Hereward brooded, blaming the King for everything, even a shower of rain.

'He takes all, and gives nothing,' Hereward said to himself. 'He even takes the little lass who might have consoled me for the loss of my wife and son. Damn William! May he perish!'

For a time Hereward thought of riding north himself, to be among good fellows who remembered the Danelaw and its customs. But then news reached him which sent a shiver down his back for all his loud talk of revolt. It seemed that three of the great earls were plotting a rebellion while King William was away in Normandy: they were Waltheof of Northumbria, who held a northern fief; Roger fitz Osbern, the Earl of Hereford; and Ralf de Wader, Earl of East Anglia.

These men made little attempt to hide their intentions, but rode about the country calling Englishmen to their standards. Hereward suddenly dreaded that they might send to him after his quarrel with the King, expecting him to join them.

Sitting alone in a barred and bolted house, he often wondered how he would greet the rebels if they came to him. In a way, his anger told him that this was a chance to revenge himself on the King for allowing his wife and son to be taken from him. Yet, when Hereward thought further, he saw that the King had all the power. After all, he had Euphemia and Cnut. They were like hostages in his hands. If Hereward joined the rebels, then he might never see his wife and son again.

So he waited and brooded, alone, as the year went by. Sometimes, in dreams, he saw himself at the head of great crowds of men who waved axes and scythe-blades, and shouted 'Down with the Norman!' But always, when morning came, he felt a little confused and also ashamed of himself that by leading the rebellion even in his dreams he might be putting his family in danger.

Sitting by the hearth-fire, attended only by an old woman who brought him food and swept out the hovel, Hereward came more and more to think of himself as finished. 'I am as useless as a broken sword,' he said to himself. 'Nay, even more useless—for a handy man can put an old sword on the anvil, and beat it into a hedging-knife.'

Then at dusk one day a rider came to the steading, his horse blown, his mail caked with mud and rust.

151

At first Hereward thought the man came from the rebel earls, and hesitated about opening the gate until the horseman called out loudly, 'In the King's name, Baron, let me in. I have ridden too far to play hide-and-seek now. I carry half the mud of Normandy on my legs and back; and I have worn out three horses to get here.'

'What does the King want with me?' asked Hereward, as he drew the bolts.

The man almost flung a letter at him and said, 'This parchment. I know no more. I am a soldier and do as I am told. I cannot read. Where is the stable?'

Hereward sat on a horse-trough and opened the letter. His fingers could barely manage the great seal; but in the end he broke it. The crabbed black writing was hard to read, for it had been set down in haste, it seemed, by some overworked scrivener. As through a mist, Hereward read the clustered words.

'Baron,' it said, 'as in life there are bad hours in every good day, so there are words in this letter which may mar the joy which the rest was hoped to bring.

'First, I must tell you that the Queen is gravely ill with a disease from the East. It is of her that I now think constantly, setting aside all considerations of my kingdom. I would to God that you were here; yet if you came, you would arrive too late. I must break it to you that the Lady Euphemia, ever faithful to her mistress, has already gone to God with this same illness. My ill news shall be brought to you by the fastest rider I can find. Yet by the time he puts this message in your hands, it will be too late for you to consider journeying to Normandy. But I promise you, your lady shall receive all the honours her quality deserves.

'I grieve with you, my friend, and hope that this shared misfortune shall bind us the closer together, forgetting all quarrels and differences. In token of which, it shall be my first duty to return your son to you, that he may in some measure make up for your loss.

'Further, since in my absence England lies to the care of the archbishop, and since a man of the Church may be weak where a soldier would be strong, and since in my realm there are to my certain knowledge great men who intend to profit by my absence, I offer you a further token of my trust. I command you, in my absence, be it short or long, to stand at the right hand of my Regent Archbishop Lanfranc, or, should his health fail, beside his appointed successor, the Bishop Geoffrey of Coutances.

'The services you render shall not be forgotten.'

Hereward pored over the parchment three times, lest he had missed anything in his clumsy reading. His eyes filled with tears. On one small sheet—great honour, and an even greater grief.

Later, after he had fed the rider, he sent for Alfgeir, the blacksmith, and said, 'Friend, my son is coming home at last. Fetch the women of the village to make ready the manor house. Tell all the folk that things shall be put to rights again. All shall be as it once was. I shall send for my knights before the week is out.'

Alfgeir nodded his shaven head and said, 'Now you are talking like a baron again, master. That's what I like to hear, an Englishman who can be as good a baron as any Norman!'

He went away whistling. Hereward walked in his tangled orchard and leaned against a moss-grown apple-tree, his forehead resting on his forearm. It was hard for him to make sense out of his life. The world seemed too muddled and twisted, like the boughs of his orchard-trees, for a man to find a clear path through it.

'And God,' thought Hereward; 'what does He want us to do? What lesson is He trying to teach us? There seem to be so many lessons—and all being given in one breath.'

30. Cnut

AT LAST Hereward put aside his grief and set about calling up an army of able-bodied men, as a baron must at his king's command. All free men who did not rise at the call were threatened that henceforth they should be known as *nithing*, or outside all law—like a cat or a dog, or a wolf. Then any man could kill them and take their belongings.

Hereward had little heart for this—or, indeed, for anything. It was a matter of form, and he had no intention of setting the army on to the three earls. So, after they had assembled, and Hereward had inspected them and sent word to the Regent that they were armed, he packed the men off home and told them to wait for a summons, which he never meant to send in any case. The King's men were doing well enough against the rebels as it was: the Bishop of Worcester and the Abbot of Evesham, together with the Barons Urse d'Abitot and Walter de Lacy had got arrogant young fitz Osbern penned in beyond the River Severn, so that he could not join his comrades. Earl Ralf, defeated at Cambridge by armies under the Bishops of Bayeux and Coutances, had locked himself in Norwich Castle and was raving like a mad thing that the world had forsaken him.

As for the great Earl Waltheof—he sent despairing word to Hereward, begging him to join them, and then, suddenly, his heart failed him and he gave himself up to Archbishop Lanfranc, the Regent.

Lanfranc, unwilling to punish the Earl in case he himself did wrong, sent Waltheof under strong guard to Normandy, to make his own peace with King William.

Hereward heard all this, sitting beside his reeve at the Hundred Court, and hearing the claims and complaints of his knights and tenants.

Once he said to the reeve, 'Dag, you could administer this part of England without my help. I am a useless old man and only get in your way. I think I will travel to Scotland, or back to Norway. The north suits me better, and I would like to see how my old comrades are faring, if they are still living.'

Dag the reeve answered, 'Baron, at the age of fifty-six, you are still strong. There is no other man south of the Humber who can handle an axe, or sit a charger, as you can. The King does right to trust to you; and you would do wrong to leave your manor at this time. Besides, one day your son, Cnut, will come riding home, and it would be a sad day for him to come back to an empty house with no father there.'

Hereward said no more. In his heart he had lost faith with all men; and he no longer believed that Cnut would ever come home, now that his mother was dead.

But he was wrong. One blustering evening when the rush-lights were flickering and the lowing cattle were jostling through the manor yard, turning the place into a sea of mud, Cnut came home on a bedraggled palfrey, and escorted by a score of knights from Montreuil. They could speak no word of English, but young Cnut had by now become so much the linguist that he had no difficulty in jesting with them, or in rounding on them in good set terms when the occasion arose.

Hereward gazed at his son, who was a big boy for his fourteen years, and then put his arms about him. Cnut smiled sideways at his knights, and freed himself as soon as he could.

Later, sitting with his father, Cnut said, 'My prince, Robert Curthose, has knighted me, Baron. He promises that I shall ride beside him on the right hand one day.'

Hereward looked into the fire and said, 'That is a great honour, my son.'

Cnut nodded and said quietly, 'Yet it means that I am no longer a child. My own knights watch me always, and would be the first in the world to torment me if I acted as a child now.'

Hereward said, 'I understand, Cnut. So it would be well for me to treat you like one of, say, my own age!'

His son made a wry grimace and said, 'Hardly that, father, for you are very old. . . . But not to put your arms about me, for example.'

His words cut deep into Hereward, but he did not show this. Instead he made himself laugh and then said, 'Well, at all events, we can go hunting together. That is a dream I have always held, Cnut. You and I galloping over the hills and under the boughs after the tall deer . . .'

155

The boy rose and poured himself more beer, forgetting to fill his father's empty cup at the same time.

He said slowly, the cup at his lips, 'My prince, Robert, is a hardy hunter. I have grown used to his ways, Baron. He is unafraid to set his horse at any ditch or fence. When he rides, it is as though he were willing to lose his life that day. I have learned to ride in this manner, Baron. Less than this is no sport for me, I fear.'

Hereward was too sad to carry on the talk any further. It was as though his son had rejected him as an old man, weak and incapable.

Something in Hereward's heart, some old pride or fierceness, made him want to challenge Cnut at riding. But he restrained this feeling, and went out to the byres to talk with the cattle-men instead.

The next day, Cnut and his knights were off at dawn, without even breaking their fast, into the woods after the deer.

Hereward saw them go. They cast no backward looks at the window where he stood. And when they had vanished into the valley, he called for the reeve and said, 'Dag, you were wrong after all. I *am* an old man, and useless. My son has proved it to me. Let us go to the counting-house and make an addition of the revenues. I am still strong enough to hold a handful of coins, I would think.'

31. The Affairs of Princes

WHEN THE news came that the King had imprisoned Earl Roger of Hereford for life, and had beheaded Waltheof on St Giles' Hill at Winchester, Hereward was still further downcast.

Dag the reeve said, 'It would have been better for Waltheof to plead as a Norman, then he would only have been imprisoned. But pleading as an Englishmen, he should have known that the penalty for treason was death.'

Hereward said, 'Perhaps he would have been wiser to do what Earl Ralf did, and leave England altogether. It was a cruel thing for the King to keep him five months in the dungeons before killing him.'

Cnut was sitting in the hall, drinking mead and playing chess with his knights. He looked up and said, 'King William may sit firmly on his throne at the moment. He may be able to deal with such fools as the earls—but there will always be others waiting for their chance to topple him. Young men of power and pride, not these country squires who have hardly ever left their middens and seen the world.'

Hereward said, 'Earl Waltheof was a great lord, my son. He was almost a king himself in the north. His blood is as good as that of the King, or of the Atheling himself. I cannot sit here and listen to such slighting words as you have spoken. Such men are not petty squires, Cnut.'

Cnut turned away and began to whistle. His men thought that this was highly amusing and began to laugh at Hereward behind their hands.

When they had gone to their lodging and Cnut was alone with his father again, Hereward said to him, 'My son, I am trying to be patient with you for the sake of your dear mother and because of the love I bear you. I beg you, have some thought for my position in this manor. It is not proper that I should be made the laughing-stock of a band of wandering horsemen.'

Cnut said suddenly, 'I think of my mother every bit as much as you, Baron. I was with her during the years when you were else-where, leading your own life. As for my knights being such common rogues as you would make out, I can tell you that each one is a brave man, each one has faced his enemy and killed him.'

Hereward lowered his eyes and said, 'I do not doubt that, my son. Most men of any quality have done the same. But most men of quality also know their places when they are guests in a house. Bravery does not relieve them of courtesy.'

The boy strolled about the room and kicked at the stools and trestles as he passed. Then he said, 'It is clear to me that my brothers-in-arms are not welcome here, Baron. And if they are not welcome, then I shall take it that I am not welcome either.'

Hereward knew that this was the young man's quick pride talking, and so he did not answer the words.

But Cnut took his father's silence as an answer and said, 'Very well, Baron, if we are not welcome, then we will go. There are many other places where we may find a roof and a hearth-fire. The Bishop Odo would not criticise me at every turn, I can tell you that. Nor will Robert, my prince, when I go back to him in France.'

Hereward tried to take his son's hand, but Cnut pulled away. So Hereward said, as gently as his temper would allow him, 'Cnut, Cnut, my dear boy, if we are to quarrel—which God forbid, for I have waited so long to see you—then let it be about something, and not about nothing! You, and your men, are as welcome under my roof as any of God's creatures could be. As for going to Odo, I beg you not to do that. The Bishop is a great man, and no one denies it, but he is a man of ambition and policy; and it would not be right for one as young as you to become involved in affairs of state. Enjoy yourself, hunt, sing, do as you please—but, in God's name, do not meddle with the affairs of princes.'

Cnut turned on him and answered, 'Baron, every day it becomes more plain to me that you regard me as a small child. Would it surprise you to learn that Robert Curthose has sent me a message, and that he wants me by his side before too long? He does not think of me as a useless boy, Baron. He is a man of wisdom, and he can judge the worth of his fellow knights.'

Now Hereward lost control of his great rage. He took his son by the shoulders and shook him. 'You little fool!' he shouted. 'Do you wish to have your own sheep's head rolling in the dust, as poor Waltheof's did?'

Cnut stared up at him, unmoved, and said, 'That will not happen—unless you betray me.'

It was as though Hereward had been struck in the middle of the forehead with a sledge-hammer. His hands grasped at nothing; foam came to his lips; he sank on to a bench and trembled like a reed in the wind. In all his life he had never known a passion to shake him so, never known a pain as sharp as the one which now pierced him to the heart.

And later, when he realised that Dag the reeve was holding a cup for him to drink from, he said, 'So this is the baron who can sit a horse and handle an axe better than anyone south of the Humber, reeve? Now you see what I am—an old fellow who can be outfaced by any lad.'

Dag shook his head and replied, 'Not any lad, master. Only one lad—and that only because you love him too much to show him where his proper place is.'

Hereward broke the cup to pieces in his clenched hand. 'I will show him where his place is, Dag,' he said. 'I will take my belt to him, as other fathers do. I will drag him from his bed for this and show him what a stern father can be.'

The reeve said, 'Sit still, Baron. What's done cannot be mended. Cnut left almost an hour ago with his horsemen, shouting through the village like a madman. He has gone to join Robert Curthose in France, I think.'

Hereward laughed bitterly and said, 'He can ride to join the devil himself for all I care now!'

But when the reeve had left him the Baron's anger died down, and he began to blame himself again for spoiling his son.

Hereward did not go to sleep until the dawn came; and when the reeve looked in at him again, he seemed to have become a very old man.

Part Five

1077 - 1087

32. Two Old Men

As the years passed Hereward and William drew closer to each other, like men who forget their quarrels because they have suffered similar misfortunes. Yet in public there seemed little tenderness between them. Men compared them with two eagles who would hunt side by side unruffled—until the time came when both wished to flesh their talons in the same prey.

In the privacy of their rooms the two men behaved very differently, however. There was no formality between them. They called one another by their Christian names, argued fiercely about all that came into their heads, and even at times rolled in the straw, wrestling like old northmen, testing each other's strength. It was as though each needed the other when they were away from barons and bishops and crowds. Yet, even so, neither ever mentioned the thing that lay nearest to his heart—the death of his wife. This sadness, while binding them close, set up an invisible wall between them. But it was another matter when sons were mentioned.

In the year 1077, Prince Robert flared up against his father and garrisoned the castle of Gerberoy. Inside a twelvemonth he was on his knees in the dust, begging William's forgiveness, with Cnut only a pace behind him.

William gazed down in contempt at his eldest son and said, 'Why do you fight against me, Robert?'

Curthose answered, 'Because you set my brothers above me, father. King Philip of France has said as much. Besides, I only ask for my rights—the duchies of Normandy and Maine.'

William bit his lip, then said, 'I treat all my sons alike. It is jealousy that blinds you, Robert. As for French Philip, he's a

163

rogue and a fool. If you believe him, you will believe anyone. As for your rights to the duchies—well, I gained them by skill and not by treachery. The only right you have to them, until I lie stark, is six feet of earth. And, I promise you, that shall be yours the next time you think to sound the war-horn in my face.'

Hereward, beside the King, nodded at these words, his hands on his sword pommel, his fierce pale eyes glaring from the darkness of his helmet.

Later, William said to Hereward, 'I have shipped the boy home in disgrace. What of your own son, who was fool enough to follow him?'

Hereward answered, 'Lock him up, too. For me, Cnut may sink or swim as he chooses. There is little love between us and he is old enough to make up his own mind now, William.'

Two years afterwards, as the warriors foraged in France, they had their horses killed under them by the same flight of arrows. As they lay on the ground William pushed back his helmet and laughed. 'Fate means us to die together, Baron,' he said.

Hereward dragged the King to his feet and answered, 'I count that no honour, King!'

That evening the King sent for Hereward and offered him the choice of fiefs in Hereford or East Anglia. But the Baron shook his head and said, 'Lord, I'm no great hand at running estates. Any clerk can trick me. Indeed, I'd be much relieved if some brisk young baron would kneel before me and take my Lincolnshire holdings off my hands. They are a burden.'

William thought of these words, off and on, for years. Then, in August of the year 1086, he called all his landholders together at Salisbury and bade them take the oath of loyalty afresh. And after it was over he drew Hereward into his private chamber and said to him, over a horn of wine, 'Friend, as you knelt today, I recalled what you once said to me in France, that being a tenant was burdensome. Is it still so?'

Hereward answered, 'It gets heavier with the years. At the age of sixty-six, a man needs rest. At that age, a son should bear the burden, and I, like you, could not trust my son to bear a bucket of water—without spilling it. Yet Cnut is twenty-four now.'

The King nodded wryly, then said, 'God is punishing us through our children, Baron. We must have done something very wicked in the past.'

Hereward said, 'Aye, you burned the poor folk in the north— and I sacked the Golden Borough.'

William considered a while before he answered, 'Yet, at the time, we both thought we were doing right, didn't we, friend?'

But Hereward would not answer this. He said, 'Why ask me? I can hardly read or write. I'm getting so rheumaticky I can scarcely mount the stairs to bed at night. I am but an old bag of bones, an old sheep with porridge for brains.'

William pulled his fur-lined robe about him and said, 'None of us gets any younger, friend. And there are times when I find it hard to sit my horse. But I shall have to, before long. I am soon to ride into Normandy again. There's more trouble afoot, and I shouldn't wonder but my son—and yours—is up to his neck in it.'

He sighed and kicked at the logs on the fire moodily. Then he said, 'Hereward, this time I do not wish you to ride with me. Will that anger you?'

Hereward shook his head. 'No doubt you have other work in mind for me while you are away,' he said slyly.

The King smiled and said, 'You guess right, old fox! Seeing all these landholders kneeling today, it came to me that a list should be made of them, and of their holdings. A wise king should know what he possesses. I would like to know about every acre of land in my realm, whether arable or moorland; about every horse, every plough, every fish-pond.'

Hereward said, 'Aye, and every dog and cat, I suppose, before they lock you up as a madman!'

But the King's face was serious. 'While I am away you shall ride the land from manor to manor, with my commissioners and clerks, on this work. I can trust you.'

Hereward laughed, 'Mercy on me! I can hardly add up a wine-reckoning!'

165

The King replied, 'Your work will be to keep the clerks in order, not to do the reckoning yourself. . . . As for reckoning, my own is sadly out, friend. Do you know, this very day I have given the Atheling permission to leave England, and to take two hundred knights with him. He's a discontented fellow, and I thought he would be well out of the way. Now I'm wondering if I did right. . . . Suppose he goes straight to the French king with his knights? Suppose he persuades my son, and yours, to join him in fighting against us, the old fathers?'

Hereward thumped his fist on the table and said, 'For the love of God, let us keep off this matter. You'll kill yourself, and me, worrying about sons. Here, drink more wine.'

A little while later the two warriors were well away from affairs of state. They were trying to recall the songs that had been sung over Europe when they were boys. Suddenly they remembered the *Iam, Dulcis Amica,* the love-song they had whistled twenty years before among the reeds on Axholme the night they fished together.

And servants peeped round the door, amazed, to see the two old fighting-men, beating time with their wine-horns and carolling away at a ditty that the rest of the world had forgotten. Two old men who sounded like love-struck young boys once more, with the spring burgeoning about them and no sad memories yet to recall.

33. The Road to Normandy

IN THE summer sun clerks in black gowns were scribbling busily and bailiffs strutting pompously with their scales and measuring-rods.

Hereward was in the granary of a manor near Shrewsbury when

news of the King's misfortune reached him. A man came galloping under the arch, shouting, 'Great tidings, lads! Great tidings! The Norman is dead!' The clerks stopped writing: the bailiffs halted in their shouting and measuring.

Hereward stepped from the granary and dragged the man from the saddle. Then, grasping the fellow's throat, he said coldly, 'Come then, out with it, traitor. What do you know?'

The yeoman, half Welsh by birth, struggled with his words until the hard hand persuaded him. Then he said, 'Master, I only speak what all in the south already know. It seems that the King, God help him, has been at his burnings again. This time he put the torch to Mantes, on the French border, because of some insult or other that Philip offered him. The tale goes that our King's horse trod on a hot cinder from the burning and flung him against the pommel.'

Hereward said, 'And he is dead? Is that the news?'

The man began to shake. 'That much is not known for sure, Baron,' he answered. 'Some say he is dead; others that he lies in Rouen, a-dying. But anyway, they say he has gone from this land and will never return.'

So Hereward saw that the western shires had already turned against the King, now the news had spread that he was stricken.

He left the work in charge of the clerks and rode towards London.

It was the same in Worcester and in Oxford. Men were out, shouting in the streets that they would have the Atheling on the throne soon, and that the old English law would win the day. Even certain of the priests walked the streets with holy relics, saying that God had decided against the Normans after all.

At Windsor Hereward was chased by a crowd and only just gained entrance to the castle in time. Both he and his horse were hurt by flying stones.

The steward there said that it would be impossible to give him shelter for long, since the countryfolk had flocked into the town and were already threatening to burn the castle down.

'We do not wish to offend them further at the moment, Baron,' he said. 'So it would be as well for you to eat and drink, then go out by the far postern, perhaps disguised as a servant. This is good counsel.'

Hereward answered, 'It seems that a man may only count on loyalty if he is there, with soldiers at his back, to compel it.'

The steward smiled and said, 'It seems so, master. But who are we, you and I, to change human nature? We must go the way the wind blows, Baron. Our loyalty is to ourselves now. So, I beg you, do as I say.'

That night Hereward made his way out of Windsor dressed as an old scholar. Though his heart was heavy with grief, one part of him was amused that he should masquerade as one who could read and write—whereas, in all truth, he had found the greatest difficulty with both arts all his life.

London itself was strangely still, like a city that waited for a thunderstorm, or the Day of Judgement. Hereward did not stay there long, but made his way on a wagon to Rochester, where, as the hot sun of July beat down, he was able to get a place on a wool-barge that was sailing for Rouen.

No one knew him, and no one even seemed interested in him, once he had laid out his passage-money.

Only once was he noticed, when the shipmaster, a sturdy young Fleming, said to his mate, 'That old fellow in black—you know, the one who sits brooding in the prow all day—what do you make of him?'

The other sailor scratched his head and said, 'I'd say he was from the old Danelaw, by the manner of his speech. Perhaps some old scholar who wishes to make a pilgrimage before he dies. See, he carries a book with him.'

The shipmaster said, 'Aye, I've noticed that. But he never reads it. He seems fonder of that long bundle he holds under his arm. Maybe that's some holy relic or other. I'd like to see it, just for curiosity. Not that I'm a religious man—but, being on the water so much, a man likes to take advantage of any relic that's going.'

If he could have looked inside the bundle that Hereward

carried, he would have seen no holy relic, but a sword; the only thing that Hereward now possessed which marked him out as being different from a thousand other ragged wanderers.

34. The Priory of Saint Gervase

HEREWARD CLIMBED the grey stone steps that led to the upper chamber of the Priory of Saint Gervase. He felt very tired and very old. The steps were so high that he had to lean from time to time to get his breath back. A hooded priest, going down the stairs, passed him and glanced at him almost with contempt.

At the top landing a bareheaded soldier with his sword tucked under his arm nodded to Hereward and made no movement to prevent him from passing through the tall oak door.

Inside, the chamber was dark and its air was heavy with incense and sweat and the smell of herbs. The shutters were closed against the hot September sun. A score of thin white tapers flickered on a stand in the farthest corner of the long room.

In another corner, away from the door, a crowd of men clustered round the King's rough-hewn oak bed. They were soldiers and priests and scriveners. Hereward recognised the King's sons, William Redhead and Henry, who stood dry-eyed at the foot of the bed; and the Bishop, Gilbert of Lisieux, who held a flask of mulled wine in his hand, as though waiting to administer it to the sick man. Guntard, Abbot of Jumièges, was there, holding up a silver crucifix set with rubies, so that the dying man's eyes might see it wherever they turned.

There were so many about that bed, and all whispering and intent on their business, that Hereward moved back and sat on a stool near the fireplace to wait. No one seemed to notice him; he felt like a nameless ghost.

Then there was silence for a while, and in that silence the great bell of Rouen Cathedral tolled out across the valley, deep and mournful, as though proclaiming the sins of all the world.

From behind the knot of crowding folk the King's voice sounded, hoarse and weak, but still audible.

'That is the bell of St Mary's church,' he said. 'It will be ringing for Prime. Am I not right, Bishop of Evreux?'

A tall and stooping churchman who knelt beside the bed nodded his white head and said, 'Yes, my lord, you are right.'

Then William said, 'I have heard it every day for the six weeks I have lain here. I ought to know it by now. Six weeks. Has Hereward come to see me?'

Hereward was about to rise and go to the King when the Bishop of Evreux said, 'No, my lord, he has not come. If he comes, we will bring him to you straightway.'

The King said with an effort, 'He *will* come. And when he comes, he will not need to be brought to me. He will find his own way. Of all men, he will find his own way—unless he is dead.'

Hereward saw the great bishops and princes and barons about that bed, and he did not dare move among them to take the hand of the King. Instead he sat with his face in his hands on the little stool.

After a while, the King said with difficulty, 'My sons are here—all save Robert—and so are my barons and churchmen. In your presence I would say certain things that the clerks should set down.'

Bishop Gilbert of Lisieux said, 'Do not spend what strength you have, my lord. Let this wait till another day.'

But the King spoke almost angrily and said, 'Not even you, Gilbert, can say that there *will* be another day. I shall speak now. Let the scrivener dip his pen in the ink and be ready.'

Gilbert of Lisieux leaned over and seemed to give the King a drink from the wine-flask, for when he spoke his voice was a little stronger and clearer. Hereward heard every word he said.

'I have a mortal sin on my conscience. Set that down, scrivener. Do not be afraid. I have a sin which gives me pain no less than the wound in my body. And it is this: that I have been a man of war since my youth. Do not shake your heads, it is true. I have burned and killed all my days. See how the candles gutter! They are being blown out by the innocents of York whom I put to the sword. Do you smell the stench in this room? It is the smell of death, my friends. It comes all the way across the sea to me from that high hill at Hastings where men lay piled about their king. Set that down, scribe, without fear, for all men to read. And set down that the smell of burning has never left my nostrils since I ravaged Northumbria. Set down that though I professed to love the deer like my own children, I never took one in the chase but I thought of the villages I had razed so that the deer might run free in the forests for my pleasure.'

As the King halted, drawing in his breath with labour, the Bishop of Evreux said, 'Peace, my son, give your spirit peace. Just as body needs rest after all its wandering, so does the spirit. Think on that, my son, and lie at rest.'

Suddenly, William gave a great cry and seemed to sit upright in his bed. 'By God's Splendour!' he said, 'but must I suffer the mumblings of dotards as well as the agonies of the flesh? My sons gaze at me as though I am a fool. Look you, William Redhead, yours is the throne of England that I won with so much bloodshed and suffering. And for you, Henry, though I cannot give you land, there are five thousand pounds of silver waiting in the coffers. Archbishop Lanfranc will see that you get your throne, William. You, Henry, be about your business, weighing your treasure to see that I have not cheated you! But, for the love of God, do not stand over me as though I had lost my wits already. Be off with you, and see to your own affairs!'

So shocked was every man by this outburst that there was silence as the two princes bowed before the bed and then quickly went from the room with a swirl of cloaks.

King William gasped for a while, then said almost in a whisper, 'My other son, the fool Robert. His is Normandy. May he govern the land well. I wish to God he were here now so that I could hold his silly hand in mine. Where is he? Who has seen my stupid son?'

Hereward, in the corner, was sad at these words, for they called to mind his own lost son. The son he had tried not to think about for years.

Gilbert of Lisieux said gently, 'My lord, God will send him to you at the ordained time. Do not torment yourself so. The body can bear only so much, and then no more. It is not God's will that you should shorten your days so. Be at peace, my lord.'

William began to mutter now that he had always tried to do homage to God by serving Holy Church, by giving patronage to learned men and by founding religious houses. All about the bed nodded as they heard his words, like men trying to pacify a weeping child.

Then the King's voice gained strength once more, and he said out loud, 'Such things are not enough for God. Hear you what I command. I have caused men to suffer in my time, men who are still rotting in my dungeons, some of them my blood-kin. God would not have it so. I command you that such men as I took at Ely, the Earl Morcar, and Siward Barn, should be set free. And let Wulfnoth, son of Godwine, walk in the light again. He has lain long in prison—so long, I forget when he first heard the doors close on him. And there is my brother, Odo. . . . Odo, man of God, so-called, who rode at my side as I burned the villages and slaughtered the babes. Odo, who is bound to me in all my guilt. Set him free, though he plotted against me. Set him free, although he plotted against God himself in seeking the Pope's holy ring. . . . And tell him I always loved him for the sake of our mother, Arlette, who taught us bravery as we stood at her knee.'

At these words the bishops frowned and turned away for a moment, as though Odo were the devil incarnate.

William struggled for a moment or two to get his breath, and seemed to be tossing about on the bed, for there was much movement, though his body was hidden from Hereward's eyes.

At last he said, in a high thin voice, 'There is a knight, Baudri de Guitry. He fought well—where was it ? At Sainte-Suzanne, it was. Under the hot sun, crying my name, vowing to serve me with every stroke. He was so brave, so courteous, so rare. . . . Baudri de Guitry, yes. His hair was like gold and his eyes were as blue as my mother's. I often wondered if he were a son of mine. Baudri, who left Normandy to fight the Moors in Spain. What a fool I was to confiscate his lands, to take all he had, like a spiteful child, and only because he had not asked me if he might serve God against the Infidel! I must have thought that I was God's ambassador on earth! I must have been the proudest man since Lucifer! In God's name, give him back his lands, if you can find him! Find Baudri and tell him I loved him! Here, give him this ring and tell him . . . tell him . . . tell him.'

Suddenly the King's voice failed, and there was complete silence in the hot room. The great bell of St Mary's had ceased ringing for Prime, and all was still across the valley.

Gilbert of Lisieux said in an even cold voice, for all to hear, 'He is asleep. Let us leave him to rest now. Let us all go and pray for one who will soon be answerable only to the God he has flouted.'

Like mourners already, the men about the bed turned and went from the room. Not one of them saw Hereward, where he sat in the darkness, away from the flickering tapers.

And when they had gone and the great door was shut Hereward rose and went silently towards the broad bed. The sheets were twisted and ruffled, and the pillows scattered. The bedclothes smelled of sour scent and sweat. The air was stifling.

William the King lay like a great misshapen image, his thin hair black with sweat, his face pale and waxen, his blue-veined hands crossed above his swollen stomach. The wound the King had taken against the high saddle-peak was as terrible as any that a horn-pick could have caused. Hereward looked at the injury with grief; to think that a warrior like William should have faced axe-blade and sword-edge so often in his life, and then have fallen the victim to something which was not even a weapon. This was the irony of life—and death; this was what men meant by fate— a great warrior-king struck down in the moment of his glory when no foeman was in sight, killed by nothing, by a careless horse stumbling on a hot cinder. . . . Even Hardrada's death from the little arrow made more sense. At least, though it was a chance

173

missile, it was a weapon of war, destined for someone. . . . But this hurt of the King's, it might just as well have been a tile falling from a roof in a high wind, an oak beam crashing down, rotten with age, a branch falling from an old apple tree, a boy flinging stones. . . . Hereward shook his grey head and thought: 'God sees all. He sees men's errors, and then he waits for the right time to punish them. All men make mistakes and offend God; so all men will one day receive their punishment. Harold slew his brother and was killed; William burned all Yorkshire and now lies groaning here; I, who once sacked God's Golden Borough, have lost my wife, my son. Now, what else waits for me?'

It was while Hereward was thinking this to himself that the King's eyes, dark with pain and red-rimmed with exhaustion, flickered and opened, to stare up at him.

William's lips moved and in a small clear voice he said, 'Baudri, Baudri de Guitry! I was speaking of you, and now you are here with me. That is God's work, to bring you here.'

Hereward wanted to cry out his own name, but the King's smile was so gentle, so peaceful, that he could not bring himself to break that peace. He nodded and knelt beside the bed, to kiss his lord's dangling hand. The hand was cold and damp now, and as fragile as that of a girl. It was no longer a warrior's hand.

Then William said, 'I had a friend. His name was Hereward. There were times when I thought that the strands of our lives were entwined. Now, in this lonely prison, I have learned reason. Hereward has not come to me, though I asked God to send him. So God has answered me, and has taught me the foolishness of my wishes. Let Hereward rest secure wherever he is, with his lands and his son. I wish him only well.'

Hereward felt tears on his cheek, but his tongue clove to his mouth's roof and he could not speak to the King.

William gasped for a while and tried to sit upright in the tumbled bed. But the effort was too great for him, and he lay back again, his waxen face streaming, his hair hanging in elf-locks down his forehead.

He said slowly, 'Baudri, my friend, listen to me. I feel in my

174

heart that there is little more I shall say, so listen. Make your peace with me; accept your lands back from me, and forgive me. What I did, I did for love of you, for jealousy because I loved you. So remember me well; and I beg you, see that my body is carried to Caen, where I once built a church to God's glory. See that I am laid in the grounds of the Abbey, between the choir and the altar of St Stephen's church. That is where I wish to lie, dear friend. The prelates may try to deny me this last wish; but you must fight them, Baudri. I must have my wish, do you understand? Do you swear that I, your lord, shall have it?'

Hereward found the voice to say, 'I swear, my lord. You shall lie where you wish, or may I lose the use of my right hand.'

William smiled and nodded then, and let his heavy head sink back on to the straw-filled bolster.

There was no sound in the room until suddenly the King said again, 'Listen, the bell of St Mary is ringing for Prime again. That is most strange. It sounds more like a death-knell than anything else.'

Hereward listened, but there was no sound of bells.

Then, all at once, William the King sat upright in bed, as strongly as he had ever done, and clenching his right first, shook it before him, as though threatening an enemy.

'By God's little splendour!' he cried in a firm voice. 'Get away from me, Godwinson! Must I kill you twice?'

Hereward started to his feet to support the king's body as it fell. But he was too late. William had rolled half out of the rough bed, and his body was now too heavy for the old warrior to raise.

At last Hereward went to the great oak door and somehow opened it. A group of men were waiting at the foot of the steep stairs, some of them grave, others smiling. Hereward called down to them, 'My lords, the King is dead.' He could say no more.

There was a great rush of feet up the stairway, and the Bishop of Evreux pushed Hereward aside as though he had been a thrall. He sank to his knees against the balusters, and stayed there, his head bowed, as the servants and the men-at-arms stripped the

175

King's room, and came back down the stairs with bundles of clothes and silver candlesticks.

And at last the great bell of St Mary's began the death-toll in all truth.

35. The Little Garden

IN HIS death William lay more lonely than he had ever been, for his sons had gone to England and his barons had gone with them. All his belongings were stolen from the Abbey where he had died. Even his body had been stripped of whatever robes and ornaments belonged to it.

No men of rank were left to carry the remains of the Conqueror to their last resting-place. In the market-place of Rouen, Hereward found a country knight named Herlwin who needed money for a new horse and armour. This Herlwin was an honest fellow who had always longed to prove himself in battle, but had never possessed fine enough weapons or mail for any baron to employ him.

Hereward offered him gold from his own purse if he would help carry the King to Caen. Then, later the same day, just beside the market, Hereward came on two fish-porters from the riverside who were willing to earn food and wine and a pair of shoes in return for the march through Normandy.

So the party set off, by road and river, and at last came to Caen. It was a tiring journey in the high heat of the summer, and there were few in the countryside who willingly gave food or shelter to the bearers. All costs were paid by Hereward, until they were met at the outskirts of Caen by the monks of St Stephen's.

Then Hereward handed over the body of his dead lord, and walked like a mourner behind. A crowd of citizens ran out to meet the procession, many of them drunk and brawling, anxious to tear back the leaden shell and to look on the dead warrior's face.

But Hereward took his sheathed sword and beat them back. Then, as the party passed through the city gates, fire started up among the wooden houses of the town, and the citizens left the body to save their homes. It seemed that lawlessness had already begun in Normandy.

In the garden of St Stephen's, half the churchmen of the land were waiting. Hereward thought bitterly that these men were ready enough to gain the fame of being at the graveside, yet not one of them had been willing to travel through the sullen country-side with the body.

As the Bishop of Evreux praised William's victories and renown, Hereward put his hands over his ears. He only took them away when a young man ran forward as the body was being lowered, and shouted out, 'I am Ascelin, son of Arthur, and I forbid this burial. This dead robber cannot lie in this ground.'

The Bishop said solemnly, 'Why do you say this, Ascelin?'

The young man answered, 'Once my father's house stood here. On this very spot he had his courtyard, where I played with my sister when I was a child. Now you would lay here the body of the man who stole my father's land from him. It cannot be.'

Hereward saw the tears on the young man's face, saw his out-stretched arms as he pushed against the coffin-bearers. Hereward felt that William was doomed to dishonour, even in death, just as, once before, his coronation in West Minster had been disturbed.

He stumbled forward and reached into his purse.

'Here are sixty shillings, friend,' he said. 'It is all I have. Now will you let your Duke lie in peace, his sins forgiven?'

Ascelin took the money and said, 'This is the first payment I have ever received from the Duke.'

Hereward answered slowly, 'And it is the last. Go your ways now, for the next time my hand reaches towards you there will be a sword, and not money, in it.'

So William the King was buried at last, with broken rites, between the choir and the altar of St Stephen's, as he had wished.

And after the last monk had gone away Hereward walked out, almost blind with grief, into a little walled garden which the Abbot used for contemplation. It was dusk now and the scent of rose-bushes filled the enclosed space.

Hereward walked round the grassy paths for a while, his hood pulled over his head as a sign of mourning. Then all at once a bird rose, twittering with fear, from the ivy that grew along the high wall. Hereward turned at the sound and then saw three men, black-cloaked and armed, standing in the shadows watching him.

He stood still and made no attempt to draw his sword. In his mind he thought that this would be as good as any other place to die, now that the King had gone into the ground. So he did not move, but only waited for death to come to him, too.

As the bell of St Stephen's began to ring for Vespers the three men stepped forward and flung back their dark hoods.

The first of them suddenly fell to his knees on the damp grass and uncovered his face. Hereward saw that it was his son, Cnut, whom he had not seen for so long, and he was powerless to say a word, his heart was thumping so.

Cnut took his hand and held it for a while. 'Father and lord,' he said, 'all life has changed in the last hour. I have learned sense. I have come to beg your forgiveness and your blessing.'

Hereward gazed down at him dumbly, but said at last, 'My son, who am I to bless or forgive? I am not God. I am your father, who still loves you as he always did. Rise, Cnut, and let us thank God for bringing us together again. Who are your friends?'

A shaft of moonlight came down across the high wall of the garden, and Cnut did not need to answer the question. Behind him stood Duke Robert Curthose of Normandy, his face strained and white with grief, and Edgar the Atheling, a grown man now and having the stern yet gentle face of a priest or scholar. All wore mail and the weapons proper to great barons.

Duke Robert bowed his head before Hereward and said, 'Baron, you stood by my father when all the world deserted him. Now I see that I owe you something for that. You are no longer young, and the journey to England is a trying one. I offer you lands and offices here in Normandy greater than anything you held under my father. Will you take them from me, Baron?'

Hereward looked at him wearily and said, 'Duke Robert, it has taken me a lifetime to learn that I belong to England, and to no other place in the world. It is my wish to go back to my manor in Lincolnshire and to tend my land, against the time when my son will become the baron there. I thank you, Duke Robert.'

Cnut was about to say something then, but Robert cut him short and said hastily, 'Baron, land is but land, wherever it is. Life is more than land. Life is meat and drink and travel and exploits of arms. I have a great debt to pay you, my friend; for you held to my father when I, in my blindness, seemed to neglect him. You did for him what I should have done. It was you who showed my father the love I wished to show him at the bottom of my heart. So, for that reason, accept my offer, Baron. Keep your lands in Lincolnshire and set a steward there to hold them for you. But also take from me a barony in this land, so that we shall be close to each other. Would that not be well?'

Hereward shook his head and said, 'I am too old now for the travel and the exploits of arms you speak of. I am too weary to hold two fiefs, separated by the sea. As for what I did for my lord, your father, that was between him and me. Your quarrel with him is your own affair. You must make your own peace with his spirit on your knees in your own chamber, Duke Robert. I shall return to my own country and bend the knee before your brother, William Redhead, though in doing so I shall mean you no harm. As for my son, he may do as he pleases. He may go with you wherever you go, as long as I know that, one day, he will come back to me and hold the lands your father gave to me. He has my blessing.'

Suddenly Cnut stepped forward and placed his hand on his father's shoulder. 'Baron,' he said, 'I love you as dearly as Duke Robert loved his father. My pride has kept me from showing that love, just as his pride did. But I have my fame still to gain. You cannot help me in this. It is something I must do alone, if I am to be called a man. I must go with my lord Robert.'

Hereward waited a while, then said, 'Where will you go, my son?'

Cnut replied, 'We shall sail for the Holy Land, father. There are estates to be got there, among the hills of Syria. There are castles and vineyards and orchards such as we do not know in England and Normandy.'

Hereward smiled sadly, thinking of the past, and said, 'I have seen some of them. Many years ago I sailed with Hardrada to Miklagard to set eyes on a melon—a fruit that attracted me by its magic, just as these vineyards and orchards seem to attract you. In Miklagard I found your mother, and so I came to have you. If you go back there, you will, in a way that only God can understand, be giving back something of what I took from the East.'

Cnut said, 'So you do not forbid me to go, father?'

Hereward shook his head and said, 'I am a tired man, my son. The best of my days are gone, and the best of my strength. I have no power to forbid you anything. Go, if you wish, and may God guide you to the end of your journey. Come back to Lincolnshire if it is his wish. That is all I have to say.'

He sat down on a stone urn that was set near the ivy-clad wall; his heart was beating slowly now, as though all the force had gone from it. It went as an old and broken-winded horse trots, sometimes with a jolt, then dreadfully slow, as though it might stop at any moment and fall in the roadway. Hereward reached up and loosened the collar of his tunic so that he might breathe more easily.

Then Edgar the Atheling stood close to him and said in his quiet scholar's voice, 'Baron, the world you know will change very shortly. I, who have known many changes in my life, can see this. England will soon be torn again with strife, for now there are two princely dogs to fight over the one bone the Conqueror has left. If you return to your manor, things may not always be as peaceful as you wish. That will grieve you, trying to hold together a few acres of land against the ravages of young dogs, hungry for fame. I ask you, Baron, will you sail with us for the Holy Land? Will you forget manors and kings and the sowing of seed and the harvesting of grain? These are empty things. Come with us and make your pilgrimage. Come with us to Jerusalem and stand up before God's altar with only what you carry on your body, as a true knight should. Come with us.'

Then Cnut and Duke Robert knelt before Hereward and said, 'Yes, come with us on this pilgrimage.'

Hereward was so moved by these words that the blood seemed to leave his heart altogether and a mist swept before his eyes and cut out the sight of the garden and the ivy-clad wall and the tall square tower of the Abbey Church. He felt himself falling backwards, as though the wall had gone from his back, and as though a great hand was lifting him into the air. The moonlight shone strongly through his closed eyelids, and coming quickly nearer and nearer he heard the sound of many voices singing, rising in a high chant to the praise of God. It was as though all Jerusalem had come into the little garden of St Stephen to sing of the Creation. Hereward remembered the choir in the great palace of the Emperor at Miklagard, and for a moment he almost thought Euphemia was there beside him, smiling with him at the music the choir-boys made.

He reached out with both hands, to touch his son, and Duke Robert, and even the cold, remote, sad Atheling.

He said at last, 'I would like to come with you, my sons. Yes, I would dearly like to come and explain to God how I came to sack the Golden Borough. Then he might understand, hearing me speak the words. When do you set off? Is it tomorrow, lads, with the dawn, the cool and golden dawn?'

But the three men in the garden did not hear these words, for they were spoken only in Hereward's head. True, they saw his pale lips move, as though he gasped for air. And they saw his hands come out suddenly, as though he grasped for support.

Then the Atheling sprang to him and kept his body from falling to the ground.

At last the Prince said, 'My grandfather, Edmund Ironside, was such a man as this. Hereward is the stuff of which the Gods make kings, when it pleases them.'

Cnut was kneeling on the grass now, his face in his hands. At last Duke Robert said gently, 'I will go inside and tell the Abbot what has happened. If it is his will, then Hereward shall lie beside his lord, my father, between the altar and the choir. There is room for the two of them, and it is meet that warriors should be together in their last sleep.'

So he turned and went into the shadows, towards where a little light burned in the sacristy. Then the Atheling let Hereward's cold body sink back against the ivy-clad wall, and went to console Cnut, whose pride was forgotten at last.